PRAISE FOR CON

"Written with elegance and wisdom, *Consolation* is about the ways in which lives take shape and pass us by, filled with crossings at once significant and fleeting. A serene, engrossing, powerful novel."

—AYŞEGÜL SAVAŞ, AUTHOR OF *WHITE ON WHITE* AND *WALKING ON THE CEILING*

"Deborah Shapiro's writing is as finely tuned in its perceptions as Elizabeth Bowen's and as satisfyingly ambiguous as Henry James's. Its endlessly questioning interiority and ability to grasp the infinite mutability of human relationships—from marriage to maternity, ordinary friendship to those profound, enigmatic connections that don't always have a name—is nothing short of miraculous. Whether she is writing about an encounter between a middle-aged woman and a younger interloper, or between three women at the funeral of a man with whom each has been differently involved, her writing has astounding depth and penetration. It is a joy, always, to read it."

—MATTHEW SPECKTOR, AUTHOR OF *ALWAYS CRASHING IN THE SAME CAR: ON ART, CRISIS, AND LOS ANGELES, CALIFORNIA*

"Reading any of Shapiro's slim, gem-like novels is like sitting down to a quietly refined feast. She possesses a deep linguistic and psychological sensitivity so finely honed, so aware of its relationship to time and culture, it makes each book feel like nothing less than a classic; these are people and places we have always known, have always been, and yet they surprise us still, asking again and again the best of questions: What is a life, after all? Absolutely seamless in its construction and blisteringly intelligent in its execution, supremely elegant and exquisitely felt, *Consolation* is yet another proof that Shapiro is among the finest writers alive."

—MARYSE MEIJER, AUTHOR OF *THE SEVENTH MANSION* AND *RAG*

"Deborah Shapiro's keen wit and deep compassion give her a dazzling grasp of her complex, passionate characters."

—SAM LIPSYTE, AUTHOR OF *HARK* AND *THE ASK*

CONSOLATION

CONSOLATION

DEBORAH SHAPIRO

B-SIDE EDITIONS

B-side Editions
Chicago, Illinois

This is a work of fiction. Names, characters, places, and incidents in this novel are either the product of the author's imagination or are used fictitiously.

FIRST EDITION

Design and layout by Lindsay Lake, Bookmobile Design and Digital Publisher Services, Minneapolis, Minnesota.

Printed on acid-free recycled paper in the United States of America

ISBN: 978-0-578-28908-3

Library of Congress Control Number: 2022937013

JUSTINE

I SHOULDN'T BE HERE, she thought.

A space filled with light, but not gleaming. An autumnal mood, even in summer. On the white walls hung paintings and photographs, some of which she recognized, and a stretch of windows gave out onto rooftops and water towers, a span of the Manhattan Bridge. It was one of those downtown lofts made habitable forty years ago and not updated much since. You might go by on the sidewalk below and never know all that existed above you.

I shouldn't be here.

But here she was, just as the guests were starting to assemble and take seats. All she had to do, now that it was too late to leave, was find an empty spot, preferably in one of the rows near the back. The crowd was mostly of an indeterminate age, somewhere over thirty and under fifty—like her—though there was an older element, too, and it was their presence, Justine felt, that solidified her sense of having entered an exclusive world that operated with an indifference to her own.

"Wine or water?" The question came from a gaunt woman whose angular glasses, black caftan, and coarse red hair gave her an oracular look, and whose sudden appearance at Justine's side contributed to the effect. Drinks to make the atmosphere more celebratory than somber—it would be that kind of memorial service. Though Justine said *water, please,* and the woman gave her water before moving along, she sat in the nearest chair and cupped the glass as if it were a potent elixir.

Like Alice coming upon the little bottle with the label around its neck. *Drink me.*

Up front, a tall and slightly stooped man stood to speak, and the murmuring crowd went quiet.

"Hello, people."

He introduced himself as Alex Greenman and welcomed them all to his home. Alex Greenman. Not too long ago, Justine had gone with her husband to a retrospective of Alex Greenman's early street photography, his mid-career portraiture, and his later landscapes. She'd seen portraits of the man himself, clearly taken some time back, when his eyes weren't quite so pouchy, the folds around his mouth not nearly as deep. Hands in pockets, he'd accrued a shuffling appeal, a schlumpiness, that could only be mistaken for modesty by someone very innocent, who wouldn't recognize it as earned, as the outward expression of an understated power. Alex Greenman, the famous photographer.

Down the rabbit hole I've gone. She took a sip.

"We all knew and loved James Driscoll."

Yes. I knew him. I must have loved him, too, in a way.

"What a loss. What a loss." Greenman swallowed. "I'm not much of a speaker . . ." He paused, shook his head, and Justine couldn't help but think that the hesitation, genuine as it might have been, had the effect of suggesting that what he lacked in rhetorical skill he made up for in another realm, his visual acuity. "But I wanted to thank you all for coming and say a few words. Many of you know my wife, Susan"—he nodded to the woman with the wild red hair, now sitting up close. "I don't know that we thought of James as a son. And I don't want to presume to know how he felt about us. But we certainly were devoted to him. Right, Holly?" He nodded to yet another woman, one Justine couldn't completely make out through the rows of mourners. "Holly, James's aunt, is a very dear friend of mine. She brokered the deal, you could say, between me and James, when he grew up and came to

New York. You know, I thought as a favor to Holly I'll meet with this kid and give him some avuncular advice. Introduce him to a few people. That'll be that." Soft, rueful laughter from those seated, a collective release. "But that wasn't that." Greenman spoke of James's talent and drive, how it made him feel, in comparison, like a privileged dilettante, but also made him excited, again, about photography itself. That James would have gone on to do such vital work, though what he'd already accomplished was important and lasting. "I hope he knew that. I think he did. He was more than his work, though. So, I want this to be an opportunity for anyone, for everyone here, to say something, if they'd like. To share, to remember the time you spent with him. To make a toast if you wish. Okay?" He raised his hands, ducked his head of gray yet still thick hair.

Okay. Okay!—a growing energy in the room, a rising to Greenman's request—as he opened the floor. A hint of raucousness, of what this could become, given the large personalities in attendance. Justine listened as a parade of those personalities—other photographers, editors, activists, news people, art people—offered their recollections and condolences to each other. A rumpled man with lizard eyes spoke of being on assignments with James in Ukraine, in Tunisia, in New Orleans, and how James had a habit, wherever they were, of seeking out the local dessert, as if partaking of a culture's minor indulgences would yield a protective effect. The director of an environmental justice organization recalled, in croaky tones, James at an awards ceremony. You'd never have guessed, she said, how much this low-key, in-the-streets guy liked himself in a well-cut suit. He didn't particularly want the award, but he kept the suit.

Did any of this square with the person Justine had known— however briefly, however indefinably? Did it need to? She wasn't sure. She wasn't even sure what had drawn her here, only that it had seemed compulsory when she'd discovered the details for the memorial service online. She and James had shared one winter weekend long ago in New England, when they were kids. And then they'd been here, on these Lower East Side streets, in their early twenties, almost younger than when they were children, more unknowing, though maybe it only felt like that in retrospect. He'd gone ahead and made a name for himself—she'd seen it in publications over the years, made note of it each time, occasionally acknowledged a certain pride in his accomplishments and a gauzy disappointment in herself, but she hadn't registered just how much of a name he'd made, really, until now, here in Alex Greenman's loft. She had made something else for herself—a life, you might argue—but hardly a name.

When the crowd's focus began to wane, a man around James's age, Justine's age, stood to speak. Rafael, he said, re-kindling their attention. At intervals he would run his hand through his black hair and rest it on the back of his neck. A motion you might make when alone or deep in concentration. He brought up what sounded like some sort of performance art project that he, Rafael, had done, that other people there seemed to be aware of, and how James had thought it was "a little slick" and "kind of obvious." People laughed. Someone, in mock defense of Rafael, yelled: "Fuck James!" And Rafael, his hand in his hair again, smiled. He'd loved his friend for that. He'd miss his friend for that.

Before sitting, Rafael gestured to a young woman named Marina and asked if she'd like to speak. No? He let it go and the speeches were soon wrapped up. But Marina was in Justine's line of sight now, and Justine recognized her from her picture. Pictures, plural. Because of course Justine had found pictures. When she'd read about James's death, stumbled upon it between a cat meme and outrage over a TV show plot point, she'd quickly lost herself in a spiral of images: pictures of James and pictures of him and Marina—clearly his signifi-cant other—a woman, late twenties, maybe very early thirties, with long, chestnut hair, bangs skimming her large eyes, a wide mouth and slightly crooked teeth revealed in candid smiles on a mountaintop and a desert camping trip. In what looked to be a professional shot she wore a navy silk dress. What an interesting young lawyer might wear when not in court. But in another, Marina, in a pencil skirt and a stylishly ragged t-shirt, stood in a small lecture hall. There were other people in the shot, a woman by a microphone, about to read from a book. Not a lawyer, then? Possibly a writer, Justine gathered, after more digging. It wasn't until Justine found a photo of Marina in the background at a wedding, looking bored, that she realized how deep she'd gone.

Odd, wasn't it, that, except for Rafael, no one here had so much as mentioned Marina? Now that Justine had seen her, she only wanted to keep looking; to reconcile this woman with the woman in the images. Marina-in-life: maybe a little more vulnerable because she was out of her element here, at this moment? Self-contained but unfocused, unanchored, slowly floating wherever the waves might take her. Once people started moving around again, Justine kept glancing at her, as politely and inconspicuously as she could. Marina's green dress, modest from the front but with a geometric cutout that revealed her lower back; shapes and color planes that brought Ellsworth Kelly to mind, and at the same time, Justine saw bare skin that made her furtive and self-conscious; she didn't wear clothes like that anymore. Marina dressed with a confidence that conflicted with the way she seemed a little lost. Eyes that didn't settle for long on any object until, that is, they landed on Justine. Caught Justine looking, leading Justine to hastily turn toward a painting on the wall behind her, wishing the abstraction of shimmering pastels might instantly absorb her. The work looked familiar to her—the violence with which thick slashes of paint bled into, or rather out of and off the canvas—something she'd once studied, though the name of the artist escaped her.

"Do I know you?" A woman's voice next to Justine, requesting a reply. The green dress. Marina.

"Oh, no, I don't think we've met. I'm Justine. I'm an old acquaintance of James's." Old acquaintance. That was the best way to put it, wasn't it?

"I'm Marina. I was his girlfriend. Ex-girlfriend."

"I'm so sorry," said Justine, coming to some understanding of why Marina hadn't spoken or been spoken of, and climbing out of the gap she had fallen into—between the Internet and life not lived online. Struck, too, by how the green-grey depth of Marina's eyes hadn't come through in any of the many photos she'd scrolled through. "For your loss."

"Thank you."

Together they gazed at the painting in silence. Not an easy silence—Marina seemed to control it, as if commanding Justine to say something. Why had Marina approached her? Not with suspicion or even much expectation, it seemed, but if Marina was still a little dazed, she was also searching, so that Justine felt obliged to give something to her. An offering.

"I probably shouldn't even be here," she said. "But . . ."

"How did you know James?" Marina asked. Direct, though not aggressive. Justine had opened herself up to a question and Marina had asked.

"I met him when we were kids. Through a family we both knew. The Kanes?"

Marina nodded and turned, looking Justine up and down the way a child might, brazen but uncritical, and sipped her glass of wine while she let her other arm, which had been wrapped snug around her center, fall to her side. Justine wished she'd held on to her own glass from earlier, her elixir-water, if only to have something to do with her hands.

"And then we knew each other here, in New York," Justine continued. "But we fell out of touch. Nothing dramatic, just what happens, over time, you know?"

"Sure. Of course."

"And it was a long time ago, now, since we knew each other. But I read about what happened and I heard about this"—she gestured to the interior of the loft—"Anyway, I'm so sorry, I can't quite believe it, and now that I'm hearing how it sounds, talking to you, I'm thinking I should go. I really don't know anybody here."

"Well, I do know people here. But I don't really know how to talk to any of them. Maybe Holly, James's aunt." Marina pointed out the woman in conversation with Alex Greenman, her silver-streaked hair pulled up loosely on top of her head, though the looseness only brought out a leanness in her face and in her body, a long-lined elegance. "And Rafael, the guy who spoke at the end of the service." Her eyes located him in the room, but she didn't point this time and she shifted her glance to the floor before looking back to Justine.

"These occasions—" Justine started. "These sort of ceremonies or rituals are supposed to provide some comfort but they can also make you feel so strange, right? Maybe it's just weird to me because the way James and I knew each other was weird."

"How so?"

"It didn't really fit into any category? And it was for so brief a time, years ago."

It wouldn't take much for Marina to infer that Justine had slept with James. But then, what to make of the inference? And "years ago"—the contrast with Marina's relative youth. She would barely have been a teenager when Justine and James had had that "brief" time in their early twenties.

"I think I get that," said Marina. "Those uncategorizable things are probably the ones that stick with you even more, in a way, because you don't really know what to do with them."

"Yes."

"I *had* a category—girlfriend. But we'd ended things so soon before he died and now it seems like there's no category

I can fit my feelings into." She drank more wine. Justine watched her eyes lower to the glass.

"I don't know that you need to," Justine suggested.

"If I don't do it, though, then it's done *for* me. I made myself read the obituaries. I'm not mentioned in any of them. His colleagues are, his mentors, the prizes he won." Marina scanned the thinning groups of people still gathered in the loft. "Only one even included his aunt Holly, just to say that he was survived by her. Officially, for the record, I might as well have never been part of his life."

Not all that surprising, but what to say? *That sort of thing doesn't matter?* Untrue. *Something about stories and who controls the telling?* Convoluted, too theoretical, possibly patronizing. Nothing she could think of seemed correct or helpful.

Marina stared at the painting, stared *into* the painting, before looking back at Justine, who still hadn't come up with a good response.

"So, you knew each other when?" Marina asked. "Around the time he first moved to New York?"

"Yeah, it would have been around then."

Marina waited, as if it were her turn now to contemplate what to say next, and as Justine wondered if she should speak, should fill the void, it struck her that she was also doing something else: beginning to establish the terms and contours of communication with this woman. If there would be terms and contours, though, they would have to wait, Justine realized, looking at her watch, startled. She was Alice and the White Rabbit now, rolled into one.

"Oh, I gotta run or I'll be late to pick up my son at daycare."

"Really?" Marina's face shifted into a hesitant, incredulous smile.

"What?"

"It's just that the couple of friends of mine who have a kid, I don't think they'd have the time and ability to randomly turn up at memorial services they weren't really invited to."

"Well, I don't do this regularly." Justine laughed.

"No. Right. Of course."

And then—Establishing contours? Because she owed something to Marina for having found her and acknowledged her? Guilt at running out on this drifting young woman?—Justine impulsively offered, if it wouldn't be too much, no pressure or anything, to meet up at some other time soon, if Marina would like to keep talking.

"I don't know, I could give you my number if you want?" She couldn't quite keep an exhilarated tremor out of her voice.

Marina smiled, with less hesitancy this time, and took out her phone.

Outside, the effect of the elixir fading, Justine headed for the train at Canal Street and considered how rash she'd just been. Giving her number, pushing her number, onto a stranger. How out of character. Or was it rather like an old character, a character she'd once been? All those years ago, writing her number down for James on a scrap of paper, on the corner of a narrow table she'd used as a desk. James pocketing it. The two of them leaving her room in the morning. She had thought he might never use it. Then she'd wondered if she'd written it too messily, had it gone through the wash, had he lost it, was her phone line not working properly—until she heard from him. And then she thought of the times she'd purposely given the wrong number. When a guy had asked for it and because it would be, what—less awkward?—than to tell him no, she wasn't interested, she'd said all right, and switched a digit or two. She hadn't done that in a very long time. Lately, she'd only given her number out to other parents, to coordinate playdates. Is that what you'd call growth?

MARINA

SHE WATCHED JUSTINE GO, slip between groups of people and out the door, not making eye contact with anyone on her way. And no one stopped to ask her who she was or how she came to be there, though a couple of men and one or two women looked at her as she passed, the men at her face, the women at her clothes: her boxy black dress that hid and therefore emphasized the dimensions of her body, her hair pinned up off her bare neck.

Marina might call her. Who knew? She might do anything lately. As if she existed in a state of immunity. Or maybe it was a state of invisibility? Invisibility, in any case, among this crowd. So many of the people here formed clannish groups, the far-flung but tightly knit tribe of photojournalists to which James belonged being the most exclusive of all. A few of them were kind and solicitous towards her, but a barrier of grim camaraderie existed. It was, in its way, cultural—they were a culture unto themselves, and she didn't belong. So, she'd approached the one other woman who wasn't speaking with anyone either. Emily Dickinson in her head: *I'm Nobody! Who are you?*

She turned back to the painting she'd been eyeing with Justine, an abstract pool of pale gold. An uncalm sea.

Abandon ship. The words, James's words, came to mind, which went to a morning, in a room deep in Brooklyn, weedy sidewalks and quiet streets of slanting sunlight. A low-level commercial building probably not legally zoned for residence. He'd put the bed up against a window, the window a few feet above a ledge of standing water from the rain overnight. Mosquitoes had entered through a slit in the screen and their high whining roused her from half-sleep. Then a slap, his hand to his thigh.

He rolled toward her, naked and exposed, propping himself on his elbow, while she lay under the protection of a thin sheet.

"Abandon ship," he said, getting out of bed.

She would suffer mosquitoes simply to lie there and look at him. The smooth hollow down the side of his upper leg, his square shoulders. His unshaven face, his dark brows and full mouth. She couldn't account, physically, for what gave him an affability. His eyes? She didn't paint, didn't draw, but there was something about his form, the definition of it, the lanky muscularity, that she wanted to fix in her mind—so that the fixing itself became an action, a creation of her own. A way of making him hers that had little to do with possession or faithfulness or claiming. None of those words, none of those concepts.

"They got me." He twisted to examine his calf, his shoulder blade. "It's a feast!"

They'd got her, too—a spot on her ankle already starting to swell—and the moment was over. Driven out, they dressed and headed down a dark stairwell, through a steel door to a bright sidewalk.

James didn't paint or draw either. He made photographs. Not of her, though. His work took him to parts of the world so often described as "in conflict." She couldn't determine whether "in conflict" was a useful euphemism, an understatement, or a neutral descriptor. His pictures were meant to bring an immediacy, if not a clarity, to these situations where language fell short.

And they did. They did. But . . . but what? After almost three years, she hadn't been able to answer that question for herself with any satisfaction. She was only unable to let go of some lingering objection she wished to make. But! And to wonder how much that unformulated objection had contributed to the end of their relationship.

It had to do with the uneasiness—the resentment—that came over her when reading the obituaries for James. How primary his work had been—to him and to the larger world, even. How primary it needed to be for him to attain the level of achievement he had. His work couldn't fully accommodate her. That she was younger and relatively unsettled in her life had operated in their favor at first. They'd exceeded each other's expectations, until, over time, those expectations—her expectations—had changed.

Facing the painting once again, she heard Coltrane. The music of parents. Not her parents but parents of friends, which is what Alex and Susan Greenman could have been. She heard voices pass behind her in the loft. The thunk of minimalist clogs she'd seen earlier and knew cost at least several hundred dollars.

A man: *No, tomorrow. I was just like, who the fuck does he think he is? And does he know who the fuck I am?*

A woman: *I'm open, I want to be challenged, but I'm also not in any rush.*

A man: *It's for the summer, then she goes back to live with my ex.*

A voice whose gender she couldn't determine: *What would you have done, if you were in my place? Honestly, I want to know.*

Whoever it was moved on before she could hear an answer.

When Marina got off the phone with the man, the functionary, who had spoken so formally, who had regretted to inform her, she'd laughed for a sharp instant. A barking laugh, a cry almost. She'd been in her kitchen, where the window looked out onto a fire escape and the upper branches of a tree—she didn't know what kind of tree, had made a point, when she'd moved in, to learn, and then reasoned that not knowing was more in line with what the tree meant to her: Here I am up high in my own place, with a tree just beyond that gets so green in spring, so spare and crooked in winter, in this city where I've never had to know the names of trees. She was staring at the branch where a squirrel dashed along and the man on the phone had said he understood how difficult this must be, and she'd softly said yes, yes, a behavioral reflex. He went on to deliver more information to her, about the circumstances of Mr. Driscoll's accident—he had wrapped up his travel in western Africa and he'd died outside Frankfurt, in a car crash off the highway on the way to the airport. About repatriation, the arrangements being made to transport Mr. Driscoll's body back to the U.S. He asked, when she was silent, if she understood, and she answered that yes, yes, she had heard what he was saying though it was a little out of her purview, that was the phrase she used—"out of my purview"—as if to match his formality. The man—calling from Amsterdam, from the headquarters of the organization that had funded James's assignment—reminded her that she'd been listed—in the event of—as Mr. Driscoll's contact. "Yes," she said, "Of course. I didn't mean. I don't know what I meant." He'd offered his sincerest, his deepest apologies. Yes, yes, she'd said, and thanked him.

In the event of. She'd been leaning on her kitchen counter as if she might lean against it for the rest of the morning, the day, the week, her life. As if her brain had shut off communication with her body. At some point, though, she'd done it. Taken herself out of the kitchen and to her bed, by the nightstand on the side where James had slept, the drawer of which held a drugstore receipt, coins removed from the pockets of his pants that still hung in the closet. He'd left, but not entirely. He might have had to come back here, after his assignment. They might have seen each other again.

She used the phone, answered calls, made more calls, spoke to the people she needed to speak to.

In the event of—James had no brothers or sisters. His mother, Lila, had died before Marina came into his life. His father had been out of the picture since James was very young. She called his aunt Holly, whom she'd met once, a dinner out with James when Holly was in town. An evening she remembered as glowing. A candle on their table, a bottle of wine, faces, warmth. Holly told stories about people and situations in a digressive, elliptical, light even when heavy way. And in setting this tone, she elicited stories from James and from Marina. Nothing confessional or deeply buried, and yet they'd been drawn closer.

On the phone, Holly exhaled sharply, a gasp in reverse. She must have suspected some sort of news, good or bad, seeing Marina's number. They didn't speak on the phone. Marina only had Holly's contact from an old text with James, making plans for that dinner. Holly, Marina figured, was accustomed to bad news. Her sister's increasingly poor prognosis and death. But Holly: light even in heaviness. Why hadn't James listed Holly in the event of?

"Oh, Marina," Holly said and, for the first time since Marina had been told what happened to James, hearing her own name had touched her. It set off an internal collapse, the opposite of the bodily detachment she'd experienced on the call with the Dutch man. She almost doubled over before steadying herself by sinking to the floor, resting her chin on her knees.

"Holly," she said, "I told the man who called me about James that it was out of my purview. That was the word I used. Purview. I don't even know what I meant."

"You don't have to know what you mean right now."

"I don't know if James told you, but he'd mostly moved out. Before he left. We ended it."

"Yes, I know. I was sorry to hear it."

"But the man from the place called me because I was still listed as his emergency contact, because I guess he hadn't changed it, in the event of, in any event."

"I can handle things," said Holly.

Holly's language sounded good. Effective. It did what it needed to do, what was asked of it.

"Okay," said Marina. "Okay."

Holly would come to New York. She could be there soon.

"Okay," said Marina. When she hung up, she realized she hadn't offered to have Holly stay with her, but Holly hadn't asked, and Holly was the one whose language was working correctly. Who was capable of saying something other than "yes" or "okay" or "purview."

She texted: *Sorry, Holly, do you want to stay at my place?*

Holly texted back: *Thanks, but I can stay with Alex G.*

Holly added a heart at the end of the message. And Marina almost replied, with an urgent pang for this woman she didn't really know: *Please stay with me?* But she untyped it and instead inserted a heart to match.

It occurred to her now, here in Alex G's loft, that she'd told the man on the phone it was out of her purview not because she and James were no longer together, but because she thought of herself as too young to even have a purview and to have this be within it.

The ten years that James had on her weren't that large a gap in the scheme of things, but they were significant years. Determining years. Years in which friends undertook what they'd once publicly scoffed at: marriage. And when the first of those friends had a child, she wanted to say *Wait*—both as a desire for clarification (*Hold up, this is happening?*) and a plea. (*Not yet!*)

So many of the people she knew had purviews now—and she wondered if she ever would.

She finally turned away from the painting, glancing around the loft, figuring she ought to be circulating. But why? She could simply stand here, out of it, and nobody would care. Which is what she continued to do, though what she really did, while pretending to simply stand there, was seek out Rafael with her eyes. He was ensconced in conversation, and she wanted him to remain that way so she could keep looking at him, but she also wanted him to look up, look over at her, become un-ensconced. It was Holly who came over to her, though.

She stood taller than Marina, maintaining the posture of the dancer she'd once been. Graceful shoulders, a long, curv-ing neck not lost to age. Marina straightened up as if looking in a mirror.

"Hi there," said Holly.

"Hi."

"You okay?"

"I don't know. What about you?"

"It's been strange. Listening to all these people I don't know very well talk about someone I've known since he was born."

"It must be. It's strange for me to feel like I was so barely part of his life, judging by the eulogies or whatever."

"We could have gotten up if we'd wanted. Gotten in there."

"I wouldn't have known what to say."

"Me neither."

Holly turned toward the painting.

"I've always loved this one," she said. The canvas appar-ently offered her more kinship than the people here, from the way she looked at it.

"You know it?" Marina asked.

Holly nodded. She'd known the artist, a long time ago—thirty, thirty-five years—when she'd lived in New York. She named the woman.

"Is she well-known?" said Marina. "She must be."

No, not really, said Holly. She was still working, the artist. And teaching. Not showing, hadn't shown for a long time, that Holly was aware of, but still working, still painting.

"I feel like I should have heard of her." Despite what she might cynically say, Marina believed in people being accorded at least a measure of what they deserved, eventually. She quietly depended on this belief.

"Well," said Holly, putting her arm around Marina, pulling her in. "You've heard of her now."

HOLLY

WHEN JAMES WAS A BOY, Holly often had him for a Saturday. Occasionally for the whole weekend. She didn't ask what Lila would do with that time she had to herself. If Lila had wanted to tell her, later, that was fine, but part of the point, Holly thought, was privacy, mystery, even. To offer her sister a door to walk through and disappear, if only for a day or two.

Fall. October. Low, gray skies. James, by the door to her apartment, with his small blue duffle bag and his green windbreaker. Eight years old. He looked like Lila did when they were kids. Though Holly didn't actually remember what Lila looked like as a child—Lila had always looked like Lila to her, like the ocean always looked like the ocean—it was only through family photos that she saw how faces changed and how they didn't. How the resemblance between mother and son had to do, largely, with their eyes—brown and gold, long-lashed, bright—and a sly look they sometimes had.

He entered the living room, the main room, divided from the kitchen by a half-wall, where the pull-out couch he'd sleep on was closed and pushed against the windows, creating space for Holly to give dance lessons. Girls, mostly, that also took classes with her at the studio, or girls from the after-school program where she worked. The girls wanted to dance to pop songs, music-video dancing, and she pulled her hair back, put on a leotard, tights, and leg warmers and taught them. The neighbors never complained. Industrial carpeting covered the concrete floors—not beautiful, but good for what she needed.

"My favorite guy," she said to James. "Welcome back."

"Where's Millie?" he asked.

"Probably curled up on my bed. She'll come out soon. Eat some plants she shouldn't."

Holly directed James toward the potted fig tree, where one or two leaves by the windowsill had been gnawed by the cat. And James smiled. Holly's was a place where you—people, cats—could do things you weren't supposed to.

She had music playing quietly on the stereo and he asked if they could listen to the top 40 countdown. Sure, she said, tuning the radio, offering to teach him some moves if he wanted. He was already wearing sweatpants and a t-shirt, clothes he could move around in.

Self-conscious at first, he quickly loosened up, leaping at one point and landing in a crouch on the carpet before springing up again. She loved him at eight. How delighted he was by the world, how delighted she was with him. They danced until they were both short of breath. They kept going even through the commercial breaks, which struck her as potentially avant-garde in some way, though she didn't think too hard about it.

When they'd exhausted the dancing, she brought him a glass of orange juice, they turned the music off, and they watched the end of the Saturday morning cartoon run. James, who'd turned up at her place so contained and circumspect an hour or so ago, now sprawled on the couch, head propped on a pillow, his legs over hers, and Millie, as if sensing indolence was taking place without her, had come to join them, settling loaf-like onto the top of a cushion above James.

"This is the life!" James said and Holly burst out laughing.

"Where did you learn that expression?"

"I don't know."

From TV? A friend at school? Not from Lila. Always that anxiousness in Lila, a roving, restless quality. A lack—not of focus or concentration—but of stillness. Sometimes it made Holly feel lazy by comparison. Sometimes she was just fine with it.

When the programming switched to sports, they went out for a late lunch, walking a few leaf-strewn blocks to a restaurant that served breakfast well into the afternoon. Turning onto the boulevard with its parked cars and trolley tracks, James read the street sign aloud: Commonwealth Avenue. He'd never known the full name of this street, he'd only heard his mother refer to "Aunt Holly's place off Comm Ave"—Comm Ave was a unit of sound for him, divorced from any meaning almost, and it disoriented him for a moment, that Comm Ave was short for a longer name that had some other significance. How strange to watch someone learn language—not another tongue, but language itself. Like the first time you think hard about your name, a word, a sound which until that point for you had always simply been.

Hol-ly. Holly. It's so weird, Lila. Isn't it weird?

Where were they? Two girls lying on the TV room floor, in the house where they grew up.

I guess so. It's your name, though. You want me to call you something else?

No, it's not that. I like my name. It's just weird, that's all.

She hadn't been able to explain it to Lila when they were children, couldn't get Lila to go with her into the disorientation. But James was another story. He would follow her there. Sometimes he would lead.

"Come on," she said, opening the door for him, directing him toward the counter, where he sat, pulled a plastic cup of jam from a basket, and peeled it open. He knew she would let him eat it, straight from the container, unlike his mother. That was the point. He slurped it down like an oyster. They ate and intermittently talked—James once correctly used the word "whereas" and Holly inwardly smiled while she outwardly nodded, serious. She wondered if he would remember, one day, sitting here with her.

They walked to her car in the lot behind her building, so she could run a couple of errands and rent a movie to watch that night. *This is the life!* The rain that had been threatening all day started just as they made it inside her two-door, and the teeming all around sedated them both. James wanted to wait in the car at the shopping strip—she wanted to wait in the car; they could have sat there for hours listening to the rain tap the roof. Just as well to let James stay where he was while she went in to pick up the photograph. Someone she slept with was likely to be working there this afternoon.

Another way to put it: she had taken the photograph to the framing store and it would be about three weeks said the young man who'd helped her. He noted the skill of the photographer, the light, the composition of the image. It was taken by a good friend of hers, she'd told him, and it had been in a show at a gallery in New York. And then, to undercut the eager showiness of that, she added that, really, it just meant a lot to her.

What gallery, he asked. Because he knew about these things—this, working at the framing store, was only a job for the moment, he'd gone to school, had ambitions of his own. He also asked if she'd like to get a drink, and he was good looking and seemed nice enough, so why not.

"Where are your leg warmers?" he'd asked, the night they'd met up for a drink. She'd been wearing her dance clothes, she realized, when she'd first gone into the shop. This had been his idea of her. Even if it was no longer quite her own idea of herself.

"My leg warmers? They're at home?" she'd answered, as if by turning her response into a question she could cast the whole exchange into doubt and be less repelled by it.

After drinks, she didn't particularly care to see him again, but she figured sex might tip the scales in his favor. It didn't, though, and she still had to go pick up the framed photo. Worse, the photo was of her. Not a portrait, exactly, not her face, but her body, naked, from behind; she was looking over her shoulder.

She'd left his place with no talk of seeing each other again. So maybe he'd felt the same. Maybe they had a tacit understanding and this wouldn't be too awkward.

He was front and center when she walked in.

"Hey," he said.

"Hi."

"How's it going?"

"Pretty good. You?"

"Can't complain."

Then they stood there facing each other, his brows raised in expectation.

"I'm here to pick up my . . . thing."

He gave her a sort of salute, two fingers to his forehead, walked to the back of the shop, and returned with the finished work for her inspection.

They'd done a good job with it, the matting and the frame, so at least there was that. He looked at the picture and then looked her over.

"All set?" he asked.

"All set," she replied.

"Okay, then. Take it easy. See you around."

Perhaps he'd been in this situation before. He seemed to have a script. Whereas she simply wanted to leave as quickly as possible. *Whereas.*

"Thanks," she said. *Thanks?*

"Anytime."

What a relief to walk out into the rain, the darkened, water-dripping afternoon, a streetlamp now lighting the gloom. To open the trunk, she passed the side of the car where James sat, where in the condensation on the window, he'd drawn a cat with his fingertip.

Shaking the water off her arms, she settled into the driver's seat.

"James," she said. Sighing. "James James James."

"What," he asked. "What's wrong?"

"Oh, nothing really. Just saying your name."

Everyone had emptied out of Alex's loft, apart from Alex himself and Susan, his second wife, a thin woman, a filament of steel. Delicate but unyielding. That flaming hair. (How often did she have to dye it?) That witchy black caftan. Her kindness toward Holly—and she was kind, welcoming; wasn't she putting Holly up, having hosted this memorial?—was tingèd with pity. She had always taken an unspoken approach toward Holly: *I'm not quite sure what you were to Alex or what you are to him now, but I know what I am, and I hope you do, too.*

Did Holly know? After all this time? She was thinking about that photograph that Alex Greenman had taken of her, when they were young and he hadn't lived in this place for very long, and she took a bus from Boston to visit him, and he took her picture right over there by that window. The loft looked different then, but still those huge windows, the clanking radiator pipes along the wall, sheets hung up to filter the sun. Floorboards like a stage.

She had been posing, to the extent that she knew he was photographing her, but really she had been holding herself, her body, her long black hair, in the space and the light, and he would figure out how he wanted to make the moment into an image, but the moment itself was hers. Her vulnerability entwined itself with a sense of control—and this transmitted itself to Alex, too. A current that flowed between them. The idea that he, as the photographer, had all the power in this situation or that she was submitting herself to him—he was submitting to her, too. Risking failure, mediocrity, her appraisal, and her scrutiny. That she might look at what he developed and say, as if trying to convince herself: *No, no, it's good! I like it.* So, the moment was theirs. Though he was already leaving her behind. His work was gaining recognition and he had moved to this place. Ascendant. She, who'd once had the talent and promise and discipline of the Juilliard grad that she was, was teaching dance in her living room in a smaller city where opportunity wasn't potentially around any corner. The expression, in the shot, on her shadowed face: wariness on the verge of yielding.

After, when Alex put the camera down, she'd put her shirt back on, her jeans, as easily as she'd taken them off. The photo session wasn't a prelude to sex. They would go to bed later that weekend, as they had so many times before—the familiarity of it—except that night would have a conclusiveness to it. Not a finality, but a sense of change. While he slept, she would get out of bed, naked once again, and go back to the window, now dark, looking out across the city at all the lights.

A few months later, at home in her smaller city, a package arrived in the mail. He'd sent her a contact sheet along with a particular print and a note that said only: *You.*

Holly asked herself why she'd stayed seated and silent during the memorial service. It wasn't a fear of public speaking. She'd been a performer and that kind of attention had never made her uncomfortable. Nerves beforehand, yes, but once she was performing, dancing, she experienced a loss of self-consciousness; her focus took over. She hadn't performed in years, not dance, not on a stage, but the pattern of the feeling, the sense of it in her body, had remained. *Oh, this. I can do this.* She could call on it when she needed to.

She was entitled, surely, to speak. But was entitled the right word? Everyone there had been granted permission by Alex. Yet there was an anticipatory energy in the air when certain people took their turns, and nobody had seemed to particularly anticipate her. Perhaps if she had spoken, they would have had no choice but to count her as an important part of James's story. But the distance between what she felt and how she could express that in the language she had was too great. It's what weeping was for. Rending. The tearing of garments. She wasn't Jewish, but Alex was, and she remembered him at his mother's funeral, not so long ago, she thought, before realizing it had been over twenty-five years. Alex with a torn black ribbon pinned over his heart. Kriah, he'd called it. A mourning ritual for immediate family. A contemporary, contained gesture of outsized, biblical anger. He wasn't very observant but there were customs, such as this one, that moved him deeply. After his mother died, he'd wanted to wear the ribbon all the time, he'd told Holly, though he understood that would have defeated the purpose and the effect. Holly needed a ribbon for James. She'd needed a ribbon for Lila, too.

When had she become the organizer of things to do with death? More broadly, when and how had she become the responsible, reliable, go-to person? She'd taken the responsibility from Marina, and though she'd ceded it, publicly, to Alex, and by extension to Susan, she was the one who'd really pulled this memorial together. It hadn't, historically, been Holly's inclination. In their family, in their sisterhood, Lila had so naturally filled that role. Lila, the older sister, orchestrated and Holly followed her lead. Perhaps she'd learned from Lila all along, and those traits had only lain dormant in her until they were given room to grow. Listen to yourself, Holly thought: *given, grow*. Nourishing, positive words to do with generosity and expansion when, really, you could, keeping with the horticultural metaphor, look at it another way: like so much shit and dirt has been dumped on you.

Holly would have James's ashes. She would scatter them from the urn she was given. Just as she and James had done with Lila's. When Lila was sick, when she was dying, James had said to Holly that if anything ever happened to him, he wanted to be composted, and Holly had laughed. Like food scraps? Like a banana peel?

And he said, "Yeah, just like a fucking banana peel! I've been reading about it, there's a whole special process, you don't just like, put me in a bin in the backyard, but after my body decomposes, you get a box of soil. You, one—whoever I would go to—could grow things with me. And it uses a fraction of the energy it takes for cremation." It wasn't widely legal, though. Yet. There was an assumption in how James had said this, an assumption in this whole conversation, that what they were talking about, his death, wasn't in any way an imminent reality. It was far off and who knew what would be legal, if not common, when it was his time to go? But maybe that assumption was only an interpretation on Holly's part, because James continued—he'd clearly given this thought— and added that cremation was the most sensible scenario at this point and that he'd like his ashes to be scattered by a particular lake in the winter in a town in Vermont she'd never been to.

"Why there?" she'd asked, and he'd explained that he'd gone there as a child. The Kanes' old place. Remember the Kanes? (Holly remembered). He'd stayed with them a few times, and then Lila had taken him there a couple of other times. They'd offered it to him and his mother, a weekend here and there, be- fore the Kanes divorced and sold the place.

"But why are you even thinking about this?" Holly had asked him.

"Because look where we are." In the kitchen of Lila's apart- ment, while she lay in her bed in her room, a hospice nurse having just left. Holly had bought flowers—purple irises, it was spring—and placed them on the dresser, though they never dispelled the sour odor of sickness in Lila's room.

"But you're young, James."

"But I put myself in situations where it's not the least likely thing to happen."

"Why do you do that, again?" She laughed, but not really, they both didn't really laugh, and the question hung there. He'd answered it before, in thoughtful ways that Holly understood, intellectually, but which left her, on the whole, dissatisfied with human behavior.

She would scatter his ashes according to his wishes, in the winter, in the snow. Just as she had scattered her sister's ashes, only in summer, by a particular willow tree Lila had loved. James would take her someplace she had never been, someplace new. She had months until then.

THEY TRAVELED SLOWLY over the frozen ground, in a sedan good for suburban streets in winter but not built for this terrain. Up with the sun and out, to get there before noon, on highways north and then along a winding mountain route and down into a valley. They drove through towns, main streets spanning only a couple of blocks. Splintering barns and lonely silos on the edges of frosted fields.

It was steep and not well-plowed, the road leading down to the narrow house: blue-gray with a red door and a metal roof beyond which you could see rising evergreens and a lake under snow. The girls put away their headphones—music to stare out the window to—when their father pulled up in front and their mother said, with a combination of resignation and curiosity: "Here we go."

Before they even knocked, Helena Kane opened the door. Helena in a ski sweater, jeans, and shearling slippers, her sandy-colored hair in a loose braid. The thin lines around her mouth and at the corners of her eyes gave her a look of experience. The lines on Justine's mother's face made her look tired.

"Get in here!" Helena said, to everyone, but especially to Justine's father, Justine thought, and with the overnight bags they'd packed not very efficiently, they went straight into the kitchen area of what was one large, open room. Bounding from the back came a shaggy black dog the size of a small bear, jumping onto Ivy, who wasn't much bigger.

"Hugo!" Helena shouted, "Hugo, off!" wrestling the dog away by the collar, then exhaling loudly, pantomiming exasperation: *Look how nuts things get around here!*

"I'm okay," Ivy said, though no one had asked. Her parents were busy taking off their coats, unlacing boots, and returning hugs from Ted Kane, who'd appeared from wherever the dog came. He was a corporate lawyer who looked like a mountaineer on his down days. Call us Ted and Helena, the Kanes had said in the past, but the girls just couldn't. Mr. and Ms. Kane (Dr. Kane, actually) didn't sound right either. They'd have been more comfortable calling their own parents Diane and Robert. So, they addressed the Kanes by name as infrequently as possible.

"Hi," they simply said.

The boys were out back, Helena said, before Justine and Ivy had unbundled themselves, and it sounded more like a directive than information. She smiled at them, the girls, expectantly, while pouring coffee as Ted led the adults to sit by the fire.

On the frozen lake, the two Kane brothers and a third boy they'd never met played a game of modified hockey. The girls had seen the Kane boys a handful of times over the course of several years and had come to expect a short period of initial distance followed by a warming up, as if the attention they all paid to each other had to be newly earned at each meeting. But at thirteen, Justine had become more sensitive to attention itself, as something to lack and desire, as well as something to bestow or withhold. She was ready to be ignored, but the boys stopped, looked up, and called out: Hi!

Hi!

Had the boys been sent out here by Helena, too? Is that what accounted for some sense of solidarity instead of awkwardness?

There were extra skates back on the porch, said Evan Kane, and Justine and Ivy found outgrown pairs that would do. Ankles buckling, they stumbled onto the ice where the boys continued their game. When the puck slid toward her, Justine tried to stop it with her feet, but slipped, ungainly, to the ground, hating everything and everyone in that moment. Then the boy she'd never met glided toward her, slicing the ice, a quick scraping sound. He caught his breath, apologized, and introduced himself: James.

Slightly taller than her, rosy from activity, he seemed to know how to hold himself, something she'd been struggling with lately. It didn't awaken envy in her—she just wanted him to stay near her. What could she do to make that happen? He went to school with the older Kane boy, Evan, which meant he was her age. The younger Kane boy, Jonah, was ten, the same as Ivy.

"We don't skate much," Justine said.

"Yeah, I can see," said James. He dropped his stick and extended his gloved hands towards her.

"Here."

She was suspicious of the gesture. Still, into his hands went hers, and he moved backward smoothly, pulling her along, coaching her—*Okay, you got it*—before letting go.

"You're good," he said, and turned to retrieve his hockey stick. Slowly, jerkily, she kept on, not looking back, only glancing down and then up at the sky and the tall pines that bordered the lake. When she finally did turn around, Ivy was back on land, having grown bored, building a tunnel in the snow. Justine realized she'd stayed on the ice because she was waiting for James to take her hands again.

That didn't happen. Instead, a sensation overcame her, of being stranded in a stillness, a distancing by which she could see a picture, an abstraction, almost, of shapes: three figures dark against a white background, a fourth beyond them, and on a rise, a rectangle of blue-gray. The house.

Ted Kane called—Lunch!—and it all dissolved.

Inside, they ate sandwiches, worked on a puzzle of a port town along the Italian Riviera—no TV here, no computer—and in the afternoon they went back out for sledding. The adults focused on each other, a division that continued into the evening, when they headed into the nearest town for dinner (a "New American" place; Justine heard Helena say "portabella mushrooms"). Left on their own, the kids made grilled cheese and then opened and finished a whole package of Oreos—the unspoken, vindictive thrill of leaving nothing for their parents.

When it was pitch dark outside but not all that late, they put on coats and ventured into the cold to walk Hugo. Up the snow-packed dirt road and onto the paved one, completely quiet and empty. Total blackness beyond the short reach of their flashlights. They were voices and flares of light in space.

They relied on Hugo's canine senses to lead them back to the house, where, inside, they played hide and seek. In the clean, simple surroundings there weren't many places to hide—in closets, behind the shower curtain, under a raised bed. In one of the guest rooms, a patchwork quilt lay over a brass bed. Justine buried herself beneath it, relatively easy to find: camouflaged lumpiness.

She lay breathing into the space below the quilt, into the orange pocket of air, until somebody jumped on top, yelling "Haaaaa!" She pulled the covers down to see him and they stared at each other for no more than seconds, before the bedframe broke, sending them to the floor. James rolled off and away, Justine sat up on the fallen mattress. Laughter, swearing—or the performance of swearing because they were thirteen—and trying to figure out how to put the frame back together before the grown-ups returned.

Ivy and the Kane boys came out from their hiding places to help, in that alliance of children against parents. The frame wasn't irreparably broken, only detached in a couple of places, and they were proud to have solved a problem, and to have a secret between them.

Out on the porch, parents stamped the snow off their boots, and with a rush of cold air, they came inside, a glow about them, emanating mostly from Helena and Ted, and more residually, from Justine's parents, too. Hugo scrabbled around in excitement.

Helena and Ted asked a question or two about the night, but the kids were alive, the house looked fine, so what, really, was there to know? Ted stood to the side of Helena, who leaned into him, flushed, as he put his arm around her waist, his hand lifting up her sweater a little, his rough fingers stroking the soft skin just above the belt of her jeans. And this is what that weekend would come to mean to Justine: Ted's hand on Helena's waist.

If Justine's mother or father noticed Ted's hand on Helena's waist, they didn't show it. Her father patting the dog, her mother already distracted by the dishes the children had left in the sink that she, dutiful guest, would clean before bed.

And then: getting ready for sleep as if it were the eve of a holiday—busy, cozy, anticipatory—brushing teeth, putting on pajamas, gathering extra blankets, as if tomorrow held good things in store. The adults went up while the kids remained downstairs, in two rooms with sets of bunk beds. The Kane brothers in one, with James, Justine assumed, and the girls in another.

She was last to use the downstairs bathroom, and in that time, it seemed that everyone had, like a light switch, been shut off. Except, as it turned out, James, who'd set up camp on the couch in the main room. A sleeping bag, a flashlight. She'd have to pass him—had already started walking—on the way to her room.

Her retainers were in, that was the problem. He sat looking at her as he had upstairs, on top of her. Open, eager, while she struggled to keep her mouth clamped around her orthodontia, nodding, her whole body tensing, seeking and not finding a way out, speaking only once she'd passed him and with the slight lisp the retainers caused. "Sleep well!" A miscalculation. *Take the retainers out and throw them away, just get them out of your mouth, turn around and go back!* If the retainers might have put him at ease, might have endeared her to him, it didn't occur to her. Only mortification.

"G' night!" he said, pretending to be—Australian? She shut the door and lay in the bottom bunk, closing her eyes so she could see his eyes, looking at her. Mixed up in that look was a man's hand on a woman's waist.

In the bright morning, parents were parents again. Remote, safe, not at all mysterious. And, maybe because they were so sporty, the Kanes seemed even more parental, in an alpha-parent way, than the Manns. Helena and Ted, brisk and ready in their smart new ski jackets and pants. Robert and Diane in the mismatched gear Helena and Ted had worn years back and kept as extras for their not-as-fit friends. Justine and Ivy wore castoffs, too. Justine in a borrowed jacket, and she didn't know what James was doing when he came up and looked to the zipper pull, just below her neck, gently gripping a creased ski lift ticket from last season that she hadn't known to remove.

"Expired," he said.

"Oh," she said.

And before she could make any sense of the interaction, they were all buckled into cars, on the way to the nearby mountain resort. The Kanes, and James, heading for black diamond trails, the Manns spending a lot of time in the boot rental room before a group lesson on the bunny slope.

Justine paid attention to her instructor, clacking and scraping her skis, still making it down the hill, though, with moments of gliding through sun and the shadow of the trees. And at the bottom, waiting to go up again, she kept silently repeating: *Expired. Oh. Expired. Oh.* To make the words into a spell.

Then lunch at the ski lodge, the decided-upon meeting place. The Manns got there first, as if this was their specialty, what they really knew how to do well, and better than the

Kanes: sit by the massive stone fireplace, drink hot chocolate, and wait.

Justine didn't remember saying goodbye, only that lunch was loud and pleasant and that when she saw James again, he said, "New pass!" and she said "Yes!" and, after they all ate, her father drove them back to the house where they packed up and drove home. They were only staying the weekend, while the Kanes and James would be there into the week.

Justine thought of him in the car, wondering if he were possibly thinking of her, or rather, as if thinking of him energetically willed him to be thinking of her.

From the backseat, with her headphones on, she couldn't hear what Robert and Diane were talking about up front, but they were laughing at one point, no-laughing-matter laughing, and then her mother leaned into her headrest and stared out the passenger window at woods that grew increasingly thin.

The Manns never went back there again. Within two years of that weekend, Helena and Ted would divorce. They would sell the house on the lake. Ten years after that, Helena would die of ovarian cancer. Ted would live across the country with a different wife and a new child, his two older sons not speaking to him.

Justine heard about Helena's death from her father, news he conveyed to her at the near end of a weekly phone call. Remember? That weekend? She heard astonishment in his voice, for what had happened to Helena, but astonishment, too, for himself, for the fact that over a decade had passed since then. Justine was still young enough not to fully grasp that Helena wasn't that old. She could offer her father a generalized—and genuine—sympathy but not much more, and when she hung up, she fit Helena's death into whatever other news her father had relayed: a work anecdote, a book recommendation, car trouble.

She didn't reflect on it too much, but that time at the Kanes' house by the lake wasn't far from her mind. It seemed to her that recalling that weekend was like learning the meaning of a word and then seeing that word everywhere—a combination of coincidence and receptivity. It was just a few months after she heard about Helena that she encountered James once again.

A weeknight at a bar in the East Village. Like so many nights now: after work, a group of small groups that kept shifting in the long, low-lit room. Warped linoleum, banquettes in the back patched with duct tape. She didn't recognize him all at once. What came to her first was a familiar agitation, a desire to engage wrestling with a desire to hide. He would look her way, too, enough to show interest but not so much that it made her uncomfortable.

The shifting eventually brought them close enough that she could smell his soap and look up an inch or two into his eyes. They told each other their names. She thought so! He thought so, too! What the fuck? Wow. So weird. But then maybe not really? Their tone: a bright disbelief derived from self-absorption, that someone from a given, defined context might appear like this in a thoroughly different context in your own life. That you were at the center of this concurrence and not merely attendant to it. But their contexts, at that point in their lives, were also fluid, ready to be challenged. Dissonance sounded like music to them.

He was no longer the boy he'd been, though his bearing hadn't changed all that much. Still that friendly, straightforward manner—how he'd extended his hands to her on the ice—and so different from that of most guys she found herself talking to in bars that it startled her. He'd grown his hair, now darker, so it fell over his ears, hung down his neck a bit and accentuated his jaw, his mouth. That quality of openness in his face—not transparency, exactly, but quiet invitation.

There was, she thought, a solidity to him, physically, but also a solidity in his attentiveness to her.

He took his beer and she took her vodka tonic to the back, quickly sitting close on a busted banquette and then unhurriedly talking. They spoke of that weekend in Vermont, of Helena's death, which he'd heard about, too. They spoke of the broad strokes of their lives since: high school, college. They were still, then, at the start of it all.

"But what are you doing here? In New York?" she asked.

"I moved here for school. Documentary photography. I do catering jobs, on the side."

"Oh, that's so great. I'm planning on grad school, too. For painting. Or maybe printmaking."

"Nice." He held her gaze. Yes, she thought. Nice.

"I do design work now," she added. "It's technically full-time but it's on the side in my mind."

"It's weird how side jobs of the mind involve your body so much."

A smile spread across her face and she drank to break a tension in order to renew it.

No one found a way into their conversation, just as no one came between them, their bodies flush from hip to knee along the vinyl, so that she could feel the pressure of his outer thigh on her own and the absence of it when she went to the bar to get them another round. And then once again side by side, he found her hand under the table and she slipped her fingers through his. Surprising and inevitable. Or: the inevitability of it surprised her. This seemed to be the point of their conversation, to keep talking to each other so they could keep pressing their legs together, keep their hands entwined. Nobody could see it happening under the table, but then who would have cared? She might hear something about it at work the next day, from her officemate Ana or from another coworker also at the bar.

He was happy, he'd said. Happy to see her, happy to be here.

It pleased her that he'd said that out loud. How little it took to please her.

She almost couldn't take it, almost pulled away, spooked by her own happiness.

She could still sense the phantom pressure of his leg against hers even as they were walking, along Avenue B, across Houston and down Suffolk Street on a not-yet-cold fall night. The last of the leaves clinging to the trees. They reached the spot where he'd parked his motorcycle, and she hadn't quite believed him because who had a motorcycle? No one she was friendly with. But holy shit, there it was. She was—*why?*—a little embarrassed by it. He smiled as if he knew—*don't be embarrassed*—and handed her an extra helmet attached by netting in back.

He got on the bike, she got on, he reached to wrap her arms around his center, around his heavy canvas jacket. The engine roared so loud she couldn't hear whatever he called out to her as he pulled into the street. "Watch your—" In a stream of headlights on Canal Street, her kneecaps waiting to be knocked off by the cars they zoomed around, sheer movement quickly pushed all worry away, left it behind, somewhere over the Manhattan Bridge late at night, between the black sky and the water below and the lights of the bridge, into the wind, down Flatbush Avenue into Brooklyn. Holding on to him, pressed against the seat and against him. A shimmering in her mind, less than a thought, of Ted and Helena Kane, the way they'd leaned into each other and Ted lifted Helena's sweater a little, his hand on her skin.

He stood behind her as she unlocked the door under the brownstone stoop and followed her into the basement hallway with the flat brown carpet and ornate mahogany table that may have been there since the days before this home had been cut up into apartments, when the pocket doors that now opened to Justine's room had led to a garden parlor, when the fireplace had yet to be boarded up and before the parquet wasn't yet rotting where it met the windows of the street-facing wall.

She'd seen a flyer in a coffee shop and now she lived here with an actor and a bartender who also cut hair. She rarely saw either of them, so it was like living in a studio apartment and sharing a kitchen with people who never seemed to eat or cook much. She had a bathroom mostly to herself, although it was gross by any objective measure: painted-over mold on the ceiling, blackened caulk around the ancient tub, disintegrating grout and a strange stain on the floor. But didn't it exemplify the kind of bathroom you were supposed to have when you were young and conceived of yourself as wanting an artistic life? Once or twice, a mushroom grew between the old yellow tile and the baseboard. Bohemian fungus.

There was no spot for him to put his jacket, aside from one desk chair already covered in clothes. Piles of papers, charcoal and colored pencils, and books on the floor. She hadn't been expecting anyone. Was that a sign of self-defeating behavior? If you go to a bar with friends, thereby generating a possibility of finding someone to go home with, shouldn't you be prepared to take them home? Was a messy room a subconscious desire not to meet someone to go home with?

"Sorry," she said.

"No, it's a nice place." She couldn't tell if he was being kind or if it didn't matter to him one way or the other.

Standing in the middle of the room, she watched his hands as he unbuttoned her shirt and then unzipped her jeans, which she pushed down, with her underwear. Even as she was unbuckling his belt, she thought: *This is happening, this is what I'm supposed to be doing right now, just like I'm supposed to have a disgusting bathroom.* An awareness that wasn't so much detachment but a surplus, an extra involvement of her mind.

In the night, in her bed, he slept. His arms folded up by his chest, one hand almost grazing his chin, a boyishness. In the morning, she lay there with her head on the pillow and he sat by her on the mattress on the floor, mostly dressed, looking down at her, the boyishness gone. A frankness to his gaze that dared her not to look away.

What was he going to say?

He said: "I had a lot of fun with you."

She said nothing in return, only smiled, sitting up, naked, moving to her knees. He followed her lead when she took his hand and placed it between her legs. Because it had been fun. He had known how to touch her. Which so often wasn't the case. Would she ever know how many times he had driven a young woman through a city in the dark?

Daylight, rush hour, they took the same route as the night before, only in reverse. Downtown, on Lafayette Street, he pulled over at the corner by her work and it was not as if they were being watched, exactly, but as if they were putting themselves on display. He showed no self-consciousness, though. Maybe she couldn't read him. She struggled to stand as nimbly as possible, find her legs underneath her, shake out her hair, while he would keep going—he'd said something about a trip last night—eventually out of the city, onto highways, to New England for the rest of the week.

"Well," she said, handing back the extra helmet. "Travel safe." All wrong, like an insurance agent.

"I'll call you." He put his hand to the pocket where he'd placed the slip of paper with her number. "When I get back."

"Yeah. Yes. Please do," she said.

Please do?

His smile was unsure, expectant.

"What?" she said.

"I don't know," he replied, reaching up toward her as she moved down to meet him in what she anticipated would be a hug (*I had a lot of fun with you*) but turned into a kiss (*I'll call you)*, her lips guiding his, as her hand had guided his in the early morning and as his hands had guided hers, palms up, so many years before on a frozen lake.

She watched him go, uptown, until the buildings in the distance converged, until she couldn't see him anymore.

"What was that?" said Ana, materializing on the sidewalk next to Justine. Ana, whose squatness had initially led Justine to think she was going to be mouthy and efficient, when really her manner was dreamier, low-level high all the time. She'd seen them at the bar the night before and had been watching just now, in line at the bodega, waiting for her breakfast order before heading up to the office.

"I'm not sure," Justine said.

"It seemed pretty intense last night, the way he was looking at you," said Ana, which quietly thrilled Justine. Confirmation that it wasn't all in her head. Before she could respond to this characterization of events, Ana continued: "I'm so hungover." She'd missed a button in the middle of her shirt. Justine fixed it for her and Ana, coffee in one hand, egg sandwich in the other, looked down at herself.

"Exposure," she said. "What I'm supposed to want in lieu of payment."

"Do you want me to unbutton it again?" Justine asked.

"It'll come undone on its own," said Ana.

They headed into the lobby of an office building where the old doors along each floor had half-panels of wavy glass affixed with gold-lined numerals. Next door was a cavernous abandoned bank you could find your way into through a corridor in the basement, which Ana and Justine had done once one early summer evening.

Beforehand, Ana had walked a few blocks east to a hole-in-the-wall off the Bowery and brought back for each of them, in large cups, morir soñando. A delicious concoction of orange juice and milk. Dominican, she said. It meant "to die dreaming." They'd sat on the cold and dirty marble floor of the bank, amid the soaring columns, beneath the grand ceiling, sipping their drinks, as the day's light dimmed through the windows. Inconsequential and at the center of everything.

Justine was enough of a romantic to hope for a call and enough of a pessimist not to expect one. He hadn't said exactly when he would get back and she hadn't asked.

Days later—four, no five, four and three-quarters—the blinking red light on her answering machine. His voice and noise in the background, other voices, clanking of pots and pans. He lived, she recalled him saying, in a former machine shop in Long Island City with six or seven other people, plywood walls, and someone's dog.

Her phone, in those days, sat on the floor of her room by the jack and she had splurged on a long cord so she could bring the receiver to her bed. She stood for this call, able to pace as he said that, yes, he was back, but also there was something he had to tell her.

"Okay." And before she could speculate too deeply on which STD she might now have, he admitted that he had a girlfriend.

"Oh." Sitting down on the floor. Relief in one direction, confusion in another.

He was sorry, he said. He really liked her. He was an asshole. He was sorry, again. Would she say something?

"Do you really have a girlfriend or are you just saying that to end whatever this is?" She surprised herself with her directness, her measured tone.

"Would I have called you if I was lying?"

No, he wouldn't have. She knew this, perhaps because it wasn't the first time a variation on this situation had happened to her. Or: not the first time she had participated in such a variation. There was, for instance, Nate. Two more or less proper dates and now they met about once a year, an email from one or the other that said "thinking about you"— code for *let's do something that involves alcohol followed by sex*. It hadn't ended when Nate married the girlfriend he'd had all along. Technically, it was still going on. She'd last seen him in February.

It was only October now. She could expect an email in about two to three months.

She would look back on this time in her life as one of loneliness. A loneliness that conspired with an egotism, where the loneliness justified the egotism and vice versa. And a tolerance, too—based on possibility—an inclination to give the benefit of the doubt to someone with whom she felt connected, because they were young and they had time. All of this made her stay on the line and respond to James, who had a girlfriend but still wondered if they could get together? As friends? Sure, her loneliness answered. Okay, her sense of possibility echoed.

On a sunny afternoon of blue skies and bare trees, fallen leaves skimming the sidewalks, they walked south along the residential stretch of Sixth Avenue in Brooklyn, all the way to Green-Wood Cemetery, coming out into Kensington, and continuing to Ditmas Park, the large old houses with their gracious front porches, where the street names sounded British: Westminster, Stratford, Marlborough. You wondered who lived there. Walking with him, trying to be friends, for lack of a better word to describe two people who were attracted to each other but weren't going to act on that attraction going forward but would spend time together anyway, not acting. What would you call that?

She asked him to tell her more about what he was doing, studying documentary photography. He used words like humanitarian, crisis, and NGO and she nodded solemnly, stupid and guilty for not knowing more about the situations he brought up, but knowing those feelings of stupidity and guilt weren't strong enough to make her invest the time or energy to thoroughly inform herself once this afternoon ended and he went back to his girlfriend. (Did he touch his girlfriend the same way he'd touched her? He never mentioned his girlfriend by name. Justine never brought her up.)

"It's not really about the extremity of a situation so much, though," he was saying, in terms of subject matter. "For me. Some of the first pictures I ever took, in a serious way, were of my mom, just in her home. It's more about, like, paying attention to what often gets ignored. A way to counter that. I don't know. I'm sure it comes from feeling ignored myself or something."

If she found it hard to believe—who would ignore him?—she heard nothing disingenuous in the way he spoke, no false modesty. She asked him when he'd ever felt ignored.

"I've been ignored by my father my whole life, so."

She stopped him—her hand on his arm—because they couldn't just keep moving after that.

"What do you mean?"

"He hasn't been a part of my life. Ever, really. He took off pretty soon after I was born and that's been that."

"That's been that? What the fuck, James?"

"What the fuck." He blew out a puff of breath. "Right?"

"Did you ever try to reach him?"

"Once or twice when I was a kid. I didn't tell my mom. And it didn't go anywhere."

She couldn't think of what to say, besides *wow*, so she said nothing. She kept her hand on his arm, even as they started walking again. It wasn't a sob story, really, he added. He'd had a good childhood, raised by his mother and his aunt Holly.

Did he always speak so openly about his father? Or was it easy for him to talk to her? The latter, she wanted to believe.

As he talked and she listened, it occurred to her that despite any obstacles, he went at life much like he rode his motorcycle. You got on and headed where you wanted to go. Much like he, and the Kanes, had faced the ski slopes in Vermont. An optimistic approach requiring some sense that the ground beneath you was solid. She seemed to go at life sideways, a little indirectly. How she had been embarrassed, at first, by his bike. How she was a little ashamed to be embarrassed, but there it was.

They kept walking, all the way back to her place, but he didn't ask to come in and she didn't dare risk being rebuffed by inviting him. At the stoop, he put his hands below her shoulders and squeezed her upper arms, a hearty comrade. Be well! Stay strong!

They said they'd do this again. Soon!

And they did, three more times. First at her urging, then at his, then hers again. Each time they met, he offered enough of himself to her that she thought it might be only a matter of tipping the scales or fully convincing him of something—her worth? their attraction?—until it began to seem, to Justine, that he couldn't help himself, that he both did and didn't want to lead her on, and that her persistence would begin to wear on him. He'd come to resent his feelings for her. She was drawing something out that should have come to an end. Eventually, an email she sent went unanswered and she, summoning some inner, deeply cached reserve of self-respect, never followed up on it. But what she could never quite resolve was how his rejection of her— that's what it was, wasn't it?—felt unfinished. That some thread of interest remained. If they had been older maybe, and more in command of their instincts and behaviors, they might have been able to discuss what was happening between them, and what wasn't happening, and why, but neither of them had the capacity for that yet. Instead, she was left with questions—about James and about herself—and the more she searched her mind (effectively the only place she could search) for answers, the more tortured the questions became.

The days with James, and the abrupt end to them, troubled her acutely until the trouble itself became a form of company, which then, in time, came to seem like a guest that had overstayed.

In time, he became a name to her, that she would see in a magazine or a newspaper every now and then, and she would think, he did it, he got where he'd wanted to go. And when she saw his name, it had a potency for her, and some twinge of loss, but not an immediacy. His name became increasingly disconnected from herself and her life.

From her desk on the twenty-third floor, she could see, through the patchwork of skyscrapers and tinted windows, the Hudson River to the west, and if she stood and peered out over the air vent, she could look down at Fiftieth Street where it met Eighth and Ninth and then Tenth Avenue. See the forms of people below, umbrellas when it rained.

It was like floating, if she let her mind drift, which she did when she could. Though never for very long; her computer screens inevitably called her back.

She trafficked in the design of high-end advertising materials, managing teams of "creatives" and "storytellers" employed to produce "content"—visual "assets" you couldn't legitimately call art—whose sole purpose was to sell various products, some more glamorous than others, some more troubling. All of it troubling, if you took a hard line. But she was good at it and was paid well for it. Better than good, better than well. Sometimes, though, she thought about her old bathroom with its bohemian fungus and whether this was precisely the life such squalor presaged.

At her desk: the morning scroll, wishing for some bright, latching moment. *Boring, boring, annoying, eh, boring, horrific, boring* . . . until she was stopped by a photo of a man at the summit of a mountain, snowcapped peaks in the distance, under a vault of sky, winter clothes, ruddy face, a broad smile of accomplishment behind sunglasses.

And then another picture, at the same summit, only this time the man had his arm around a woman, both of them smiling at the camera, smiling at their luck.

She zoomed in on the images and her heartbeat quickened.

The man on the mountaintop was James. Of the broken bed, of the motorcycle, the frustrating walks.

She kept reading. *Rest in peace,* people wrote. *Rest in power. Rest easy. So young. Too young.* She couldn't read fast enough. These were death notices? She scrolled on and found a "so sorry for your loss" message addressed to Marina, clearly the young woman at the summit with him in the image. Whoever Marina was, she hadn't publicly responded to it.

Her computer chirped with work notifications that she let go. The more Justine read, the stronger the uncomfortable urge to insert herself. She was never sure she understood the codes of behavior here, where anyone could theoretically read or view anything, but where it was also assumed to be unseemly to read what had so publicly been posted if you didn't know or weren't in some way connected to the person who'd posted it. And what was at the root of this desire to participate in this public outpouring? She wasn't friends with James Driscoll and certainly wasn't part of his life. And still, she wished to say something, anything, to the effect of: *I knew him, too.*

When she thought of James, and she had thought of him from time to time, she imagined they might run into each other, ten or twenty years from now, and they would recognize each other, as they had in the bar that long ago night, say hello, with warmth, maybe even some inner tremble of excitement, then go their separate ways, then think vaguely but pointedly about time and the ways it passes. Losing even this minor possibility cast a shadow over possibility in general. A death of possibility. You couldn't post that.

She stood because she couldn't sit still any longer, closed all the open windows on her monitor, then headed down the hall to the elevator bay, out of the lobby, across the block to a small, set-back plaza between two skyscrapers, scattered with bright green metal chairs.

Adam answered his phone when she called. He knew nothing about James, not because James was a secret Justine had kept but because her experience with James had lived inside of her in the way of a dream, with dense and deep meaning for the dreamer but meaning that became slight and diminished when talked about. You couldn't post that either.

But her husband was the first person she wanted to call, to tell him about the weird feeling that had taken hold of her. He might know what to make of it, what to do with it, other than what Justine was doing, sitting in one of the green chairs as if she might not get up for a long time.

She conveyed the details to him—or what she'd picked up. There had been a car accident though she didn't know the full story yet. She described James as someone she'd gone out with very briefly, who had driven her across the Manhattan Bridge on a motorcycle, the only time that had ever happened to her.

Adam responded with single words and pauses—he was listening, a little guarded, a sharpness in his voice that was a little proprietary, too.

"A motorcycle. Huh."

"It's just strange. I mean, I didn't know him well at all," she said, trying and failing to get at a reverberation that seemed to be coming from both inside and outside her, from the green chairs and the skyscrapers, from the city itself. It had to do with how long ago the time with James seemed and how it didn't seem long ago at all. Adam said something about mortality hitting her and she said that was too simple.

"Mortality is too simple?"

"You know what I mean. It's not like, oh shit, we all die, and life is short, better get on it. It's more like this sense of dislocation."

"I get that."

Silence again, in which the dislocation continued to take hold, like a balloon that could carry her away.

"Where are you?" she asked.

"In the office, at my desk."

"I should get back to mine."

"I can keep talking, if you want. I can stay on the phone."

"It's okay, maybe we can talk more later. I don't really know what else I have to say."

They said they loved each other and hung up. The tall buildings on either side created a valley and the city sun cast shadows on the concrete, on her lap, where she sat, having put her phone away. Was this shock? This sensation, or absence of sensation, of being acted on by a delicate anesthetic. A drifting from solidity and a desire to stay in the destabilization. Not unpleasant, really. It was, surprisingly, light. She sat there until the sun shifted higher in the sky and she was out of shadow, until the sun began to burn her bare arm.

At her computer once again, she found more pictures of James, pictures of his work. Some images she'd seen before, without even registering at the time that he had taken them. Others were new to her. A series of black-and-white photographs of men in life vests packed closely on an inflatable boat under dark gray skies. The water looked ominous, cold. The lighting was harsh, loaded with drama, but in one shot some of the men were smiling for his camera, not because, it seemed to Justine, they were at all relieved or untroubled to be reaching a shore, but out of some reflexive human habit, an awareness on their part of being photographed. The smiles were eerie, and this complicated awareness made the picture. You had to imagine the photographer—James—there, too, bearing witness but not without some complicity, and possibly smiling uneasily in return. You had to imagine he was able to earn people's trust. You had to imagine him paying attention, as she remembered he'd once put it.

A little disgusted with herself for how deep she'd gone, she straightened in her chair and refocused, though not before taking out her phone to watch, three times, an old video of her son Oliver, as a toddler, walking, stumbling, walking in the sun, smiling along a terraced gravel path.

The evening of the memorial at Alex Greenman's loft, Justine put Oliver to bed with a sequence of books and songs, and as she kissed him goodnight, he clapped his little hand to the back of her neck, pulling her so close. She stayed kneeling by his bed as he let go and fell asleep, caught in the tension between wanting to stay with him and needing to go, even if it was only to lie on the couch with Adam and watch TV. Between episodes that evening, she told Adam about the memorial gathering and how Marina came over to her after, not to catch her out for crashing the service or point a finger, but acting on an impulse Justine couldn't quite name: not avid enough to be called curiosity, not withholding enough to be suspicion, but more intense than mere politeness.

Like she needed something Justine might be able to give. How it had led her, Justine, to suggest they get together.

Maybe there was no way to name it, just as Justine couldn't quite define what had led her to go to the memorial in the first place, just as she couldn't define what she and James had been to each other.

"Is that strange?" she asked Adam. "That I gave her my info."

"I don't think so. It's not like you gave her a business card at a funeral. And if she does think it's weird, after the fact, then she just won't get in touch."

"People," Justine said.

"People," he echoed.

They barely made it to the end of the second episode before nodding off and then heading to bed. Getting out of her clothes and washing up roused her a little, and Adam fell asleep before she did. In the dark, his back to her, she put her hand on his shoulder, her face in the hollow between his shoulder blades, to feel the strength and the vitality of his body, and the terror: that one day he would be gone.

She moved her hand up under his t-shirt and his skin was softer than usual, so that his body felt new to her somehow. He turned over, responding to her touch. And this sense that his body was a stranger's only intensified. (Had it really been so long since the last time?) It was unsettling and surprising, and yet the newness didn't completely dispel the deep knowledge they had of each other's bodies, the kind of knowledge you accrue over eight years if you keep paying attention. But the newness brought forth a strangeness: Who is this person? What is he thinking? What does he want? If he were to tell me what he wants, would it be exciting to me? His skin was softer as if the whole structure of his skin cells had changed. When had this happened? And how? Was it age? The beginning of a general, allover slackening? His body was still so strong, though. Was it a shift in her power of perception? Was that also age? One day all of this would be gone.

IT WAS EARLY EVENING when Marina left the Greenmans' loft and kept walking in the strange hush of a Friday in August. People had fled the city for the weekend already or hadn't yet ventured out for the night. A suspension of sorts that she was content to move about in, and her earlier sense of immunity revived itself. A feeling not unlike a fever, of being vulnerable yet untouchable. Out of the stream of life, where nothing, besides your sickness, could harm you.

In a bar on Rivington Street, she ordered an icy, citrusy cocktail from a menu printed on brown butcher paper. Tart, bright, metallic, and cooling: her drink came into focus for her and then her focus shifted to the neck of a young man a few stools down, all the black ink from his collarbone to his jaw. She wouldn't have labeled it desire, her interest in him, but she wasn't sure what else to call it. Her sense of immunity, of invisibility was strong enough to make her believe he wasn't aware of her looking.

"Can I help you?" He turned to face her. Surly. As if he reluctantly spent all day behind a counter and she was the latest customer through the door.

"I'm sorry." She shook her head, slightly shocked out of her stupor. "I was staring." He waved it away—it was fine. They were good. He went back to his whiskey. She so rarely stared. Because she knew better. Because she was a born New Yorker.

James had once remarked on her "placidity"—his sense that not much stunned or impressed her, not much led her to stare—and he attributed this to her having grown up in the city. They were in her kitchen, before he'd moved in with her, though even once he'd moved in, her place remained *her* place, a home base for him more than a home.

"Placidity," she'd said. "You mean like I don't give a shit about anything?" Not the way you do, she'd thought.

"No, I mean you're not a wide-eyed tourist or a transplant. And you also don't act like this city is your own movie set. It's just what you know."

She didn't argue the point with him then, but the city did its work on her, nonetheless, infiltrating and ordering her memory. Her parents' old classic six on Park Avenue, private high school two blocks away. Bricks and brownstone. Central Park. And across the park, the dark, carpeted hush of the hall of gems at the natural history museum, her childhood, gone now.

Such a privileged upbringing. People didn't always know how to approach her, people she encountered through volunteer work when she was a teenager, or a little later in college classes. Didn't know whether to forgive her, if she was even asking for forgiveness. Or they assumed some shame on her part. And Marina, at seventeen, at twenty, had been ashamed—of the classic six, of the private schools, of affluence, of disparity. She came up with contortions when pressed—and she'd often felt pressed, guilty: We have money but not *that kind* of money. Which was true, and yet she had such a keen familiarity with gradations of wealth, and knowledge of their shades and subtleties: How many kinds of money there were and what each kind meant.

By the time she met James, who also understood how many kinds of money there were, because he'd grown up around it but without all that much of it himself, she no longer felt the need to obscure how she'd been raised. She had other things she preferred to hide. Ambitions she was no longer sure she was entitled to have. Which undercut the whole concept of ambition, driven as it ultimately is by a sense of entitlement. For a born New Yorker to think such a thing! Or was it the New Yorker in her that allowed her the hawk's perspective, circling above it all, above ambition even, all that effortful scrambling?

Marina had wanted to write. To write the way one of her favorites, Marguerite Duras, had written. So grand had been her ambitions once. Marina had wanted, she now believed, what may not have been possible for her to achieve in America in the early twenty-first century. But she'd gone to a program, a good one, where she was supposed to earn some stamp of validation and legitimacy. And her parents supported this. They paid for it, at any rate. They didn't tell her, as the Duras mother did in *The Lover*, that the girl who wanted to write should instead pursue a mathematics degree. Her mother was not a Duras mother, moody and depressed and enchanting, impoverished in a crumbling colonial house and the humidity.

Marina's mother was a credit card company executive who wore expensive silk shirts. Marina's mother was not Duras's mother and Marina was not Marguerite. The fifteen-year-old girl in the brown-pink fedora with the black band, worn dress, leather belt, gold lamé shoes, leaning against the railing on the ferry to Saigon.

Associative. Lulling but shocking. Irresistible: Duras's work didn't seem to capture the imagination of anyone in Marina's courses, and taking cues, Marina stopped talking about her. The classmate she'd been sleeping with didn't care. He would go on to publish a very well received first novel, *No Big Deal*, in which the young male protagonist has some weird sex with a bit character named Mariah who grew up on the Upper East Side and whose mother was a credit card company executive. Mariah's appearance in the book was exceedingly brief, essentially there to unwittingly teach the protagonist a valuable lesson about capitalism.

But Marina's cooperative silence in class bred an inner alienation, and while Duras's ambition, and her over-the-top ways, never came to seem naïve or embarrassing to Marina, her own ambition, for herself, had come to seem naïve and embarrassing. Untenable and foolish. After graduate school, and a manuscript that would ultimately, despite a few exclamatory emails from editors, remain an icon on her desktop, she found a job—a university communications position loosely linked to her skill set that wasn't exactly taxing and would theoretically give her time and energy to continue to work on her writing as well as provide a suitable answer when anyone asked what she did. She settled into it, and kept at it, as a cover, in a way.

She wrote sometimes, which is to say she did not write the way Duras wrote. Still, she kept her copies of Duras prominent on her bookshelves, and in rare instances someone would pull one down. Like James had, when they were getting to know each other.

He opened the books to find all her old underlining and marginalia. Like a whisper: *Look*. A whisper, because it is quiet, is demanding. It presumes a listener and calls that listener near. There's some entitlement, after all, in a whisper. James had come near.

A long mirror ran behind the bar and she could see that the guy with the tattoos was now looking at her, in the glass.

"My turn." He smiled.

Okay, then. Why not? She picked up her drink and her bag and moved toward the empty stool beside him, watching his eyes go to the back of her dress, to where it opened. Where he might put his hand at some point. Standing slightly above him, she took it as an opportunity for closer inspection of the designs on his neck. In the dimness, she could make out some kind of lettering that didn't read as an actual word to her.

"Does that one mean something?"

"Which one?"

"This one." Touching the pulse point on his right side. His eyes followed her hand as she lowered it.

"Oh, that one. It's super personal. I'd have to know you better."

Down she sat.

"I should tell you something," he said.

"What's that?"

"I'm waiting for someone."

"I see." She nodded gravely. Mock gravity. "I can move. It's all right."

"No, you should stay. I just didn't want it to be all awkward when she gets here. It's gonna be awkward anyway."

"Now I'm intrigued."

"No, she's just, you know, we met on an app and we've seen each other a few times but I don't know."

"So, this time it's like make or break?"

"Not sure I'd put it that way, but sort of. She probably feels the same way."

Marina gave him an exaggerated shrug: Like, who knew what was possible in this world? And then a woman, cute, with curly dark hair cut in the shaggy style that had returned, and dressed in a zippered boilersuit, came through the door.

As he got up with his drink and went to meet her, he brushed his hand along Marina's shoulder. She was sure the cute woman hadn't seen it, but then maybe she had, because instead of finding a table, they had a quick conversation in the fading light of the front window and decided to go elsewhere. He brought his glass back to the bar and gave Marina a long look before he left.

What would she have done if the cute woman hadn't been a factor? She hadn't been thinking that far in advance. Only that his fingertips had felt good on her shoulder. Is this what lay in store for her, post-James?

An image: Rafael, standing in front of everyone in the loft and saying her name. How he'd disarmed her when he spoke at the service, so that she was grieving not only the James she lost but the James that Rafael had lost. A double, or compounded, loss. And then when he'd asked if she wanted to get up and speak, when he'd made a point of singling her out, when he was the only one to do so, she was overcome.

She ordered a refill of her cocktail, cold in the summer heat, and retreated into herself, into a thought of winter, of waking to deep snow, tall evergreens weighted in white, like giant, shaggy puppets. A frozen lace of snowflakes on the windowpane. The first one up, her robe draped over her t-shirt, her thick socks on pine floors, she'd left him sleeping under the covers of a large bed beneath a sloped ceiling. Swedish, she was told. The people who owned this place. Or the wife. The husband was American. They'd gone to live in Stockholm when they'd had children, but they'd held on to this house, left a turntable and records, left the walls a shade of Scandinavian gray-blue, the color of early morning light and the color of dusk. Being here with James was a bit like playacting. She would never be Swedish, but would she one day have a similar life?

The foot of the stairs opened into a living space with a couch, bookshelves, and a woodburning stove. The glass doors to the deck were banked with snow, almost knee-high. Outside: a brightness already, as if the sun couldn't wait. The car was buried, the mountain road unplowed. They wouldn't be going anywhere that morning.

She put coffee on in the kitchen. It must have been a dark early evening in Stockholm where, she imagined, the Swedish-American couple were preparing dinner with their young son and daughter. An atmosphere, she imagined, of security, good taste, gentle socialism. She'd conjured this picture of them from where? There were no personal photos here. They were friends with James, she didn't know the history, but they'd let him stay here this week, deep in the Catskills, between paid bookings.

It wasn't long before she heard him come down the stairs, before he stood across from her, on the other side of a half-wall partition, leaning toward her, his upper arms defined and flush against the short sleeves of his t-shirt. He raked his hand through his hair, a gesture of half waking up, half holding on to sleep, a gesture of sex.

He'd only ever been to this house a couple of times in the summer, he told her, taking his coffee to the wide window where a few dead flies curled on the sill, last alive in September, baked by the sun. The secluded view took in a frozen pond, a couple of neighboring houses far enough away that you'd only be able to make out figures, if there were even anyone about. But there was no one about.

"It's different in winter," he said. It reminded him of a place he stayed when he was growing up. A house in Vermont that had belonged to his friend's family. Where they would play hockey on the ice and ski at nearby slopes.

"It sounds nice." She followed him out into the room.

"It was. It was the first place I ever went to that felt un-known. Unfamiliar in that way that actually feels reassuring and also exciting, like the world is large and strange. And you didn't know it before but now you do. But it was so normal to them, to the Kanes. Even having a second home was so normal to them. So, I never said it out loud, I didn't want to sound stupid, I just internalized it."

I like that you talk, she thought, sitting cross-legged on the couch, settling in, to listen. He joined her there. *I like how you talk*. She didn't consider listening to him a sign of passivity. No, it was an act of engagement.

"It was formative for you," she said.

"Yeah. And my family, my mom, we lived in an apartment, you know, in a town where most people lived in houses. The Kanes had a really big, really nice one. There was this tension

I would feel when I spent time with them. You just absorb it when you don't have words for it."

"What did you absorb?"

"It was like—they were genuinely friendly and inviting. They liked having me there. But I would wonder why they liked having me there. They never said anything, it was all just under the surface, but there was this sense that they were doing something good, that they were good people for including me in their good family. They were well-off, I wasn't. But there was more to it than that. Because despite all their advantages, it was like I was better, oddly enough, at what they did than they were."

"What do you mean, better?"

"I had this kind of natural aptitude for things they did, their activities, their ways of being. Like skiing. My mom would never have taken me skiing. She wouldn't have known how. She had maybe taken me skating once or twice, at the municipal rink. Or my aunt Holly did. She could really skate. Anyway, it came so easily to me, that physicality. I was really good at it."

"And so modest," said Marina, fixing her eyes on him, turning up the corners of her mouth.

He shook his head and surrendered his hands. But she still found his openness unusual, alluring. Had he always been like this? Was it a factor of his being older than her? She smiled at him: *Go on.* He stood, as if the rhythm of his talk required it.

"No, but they *made* me feel it, they made me aware of it. I could see them seeing me. I remember one time I was just lying on the couch and Helena, the mother, looked at me and said it was like the couch itself wanted me there."

"Whoa," said Marina. "Alert the authorities."

"Yeah. But it was subtle, it wasn't sexual . . . I don't think? Maybe it was just in relation to Evan, her own son."

He went to the window, where the sun beamed in, bouncing off the snow. Marina thought she knew what Helena had seen. How smoothly he must have grown into his new body.

He grasped that it was a fine line he was meant to walk, he said, even if he couldn't have articulated it at the time. When the Kanes—the adults as well as the kids—brought him into their fold, the fold itself took on a sheen and the sheen is what they were after. In some way, it was completely removed from him. He had a role to play for them and their interest in him, their fidelity to him, depended on the extent to which he could inhabit this character. He didn't understand the competing impulses, the ambivalence—how he could want to be around them even as he grew to resent them, resent what they needed from him.

She finished her coffee and went over to him, wordlessly offering to refill his cup, too.

"So what happened with all of it?" she called from the counter.

He grew up, drifted from Evan Kane and toward other friends. Two years, three years is so much time in one's life then. He missed their dog, though. They had this "fucking huge, amazing" dog. Hugo. He was really a beast. He could knock you over. But with love!

Returning to him, then returning to her spot on the couch.

The Kanes would divorce before he finished high school and guilt would come for him when he'd see Evan in the halls at school, Evan with faint pockmarks on his face, James wondering what, if any, part he played in the dissolution of the Kane family, even if it was only the effect of his absence.

"When I told my mother about the split, she said 'Oh, that's too bad,' the way you would if someone told you they overcooked a meal."

"Did your mom just hate them? The Kanes?" Marina asked.

"Probably," he said, smiling. On some level. They weren't friends, as far as he knew, but the Kanes had let him and his mom come stay at the Vermont house a couple of times when they had other plans.

When he pressed his mother on it—too bad?—she said, Well, at least now Helena would no longer pity her or be suspicious of her. And when he asked what she meant, she elaborated: that Helena looked at her like she was contagious, like Helena might catch whatever his struggling, single mother had, but was also curious. As if she, his mother, possessed some secret knowledge.

He was skeptical, and his mother told him: Oh, it was definitely there, in the way Helena would tense whenever their paths happened to cross. The brittle pity disguising her discomfort but also her interest.

He still wondered, now, if his mother had placed too much emphasis on minor things and not enough on the major ones. Couldn't see the forest for the trees. Divorce got a dismissive "too bad" from her, but she could dwell with sensitivity upon the intricacies of a stance, of a look.

"But that's what you do, isn't it? I mean when you take pictures," said Marina. "Dwell on the intricacies of a look."

"True. They say something about that, right? Apples. Trees."

Lila, his mother's name was Lila, Marina reminded herself. She never met Lila, who had died only a couple of years before she met James. But she'd seen pictures and she could imagine Lila taking satisfaction in the ways this Helena edged around her, in the power she had to make Helena uneasy.

"Anyway, that's a lot before breakfast," said James.

She unwound her legs and stretched her whole body the length of the couch, catlike, her robe hanging open and her shirt twisting up, revealing her underwear and the soft skin just above it, and he watched her, content.

"Are you hungry?" he asked.

"I don't know. I don't feel like making anything. I don't feel like starting the day, getting dressed." But she was on her feet now. "Going out in the snow."

"Then don't," he said. "We don't have to get dressed."

He placed his cup on a side table and went to her. His face was unsmiling; a seriousness, a zoning in she saw from him mostly in these moments. She put her cup next to his, so that he could run his hands up under her shirt, along her back, before she let the robe fall and let him take her shirt off. Then he moved his hands to her hips in the way she loved, that he knew she loved. Back upstairs they went.

Sex with him was a point of connection, edged with an intensity. They hadn't grown so accustomed to each other yet. There were still moments when it could have gone wrong, some misunderstood revelation or unmet request. In the same way she couldn't always be sure if he was going to laugh when she said something she found funny and cutting or respond with a kind of thin smile that revealed her own young glibness to her. (Usually he laughed.) But they wanted each other, wanted to please each other. Over time, it would start to seem that they wanted each other in some fixed way, that they carried around some unchanging idea of what the other wanted and how to go about that. But for now, nothing had been set.

When that intensity between them had wrung itself out, a restlessness rose in him and despite his morning laziness, he could no longer stand to stay inside. He bundled up and trudged out into the snow. No judgment, though—he'd left the house in an easy mood, no pressure or disappointment in her for wanting to stay in, to lounge around. They were separate people who could do their own thing.

After a time, reading a book, an empty cup of tea on the side table, she became aware that it would be nice to have a lamp on, that the sky had darkened, the sun setting on blue snow. It wasn't that late, not yet five, but he wasn't back. It had been what, two hours? Three? She went upstairs for her phone. No notifications. She called him, knowing that reception was patchy, only to hear a chiming, coming from downstairs, his own phone, that he'd left behind.

She didn't panic. Not yet. He'd been in remote and hostile locations and returned unharmed. But he'd been in those situations with other people, a driver, a translator. Where could he be now? No phone, and he hadn't taken a flashlight with him. Not counting the untold number of paths and quasipaths in the woods, he could have gone left along the road they came in on, toward the grocery store. As far as she knew, he didn't know any of the neighbors well enough to want to stop in. As far as she knew.

Her rational mind prevailed, but a question began to buzz with increasing volume: *What if?* What if he's lost, what if he's injured out there alone in the cold, what if he's dying, dead? Or what if—heading off the rails—what if he's not the person I think he is, what if he has a second phone, what if this, and everything leading up to this, has been an act, a ruse, to lure me to this isolated place . . . and then what? The windows, now black in the dark, reflected her drawn face.

She found a flashlight in a cupboard, got her boots and coat on. She would walk to the nearest neighbor's house where the lights were on. If no one was home, she would find cell service and call the police, if only to hear another human voice. Beyond that, she didn't know. One more look through—but really at—the window, a distorted mirror of a room.

The door by the kitchen opened and she turned to see him standing there, apology and astonishment on his face, glassy-eyed from the cold.

"Fucking hell," he said, and laughed, in relief, it seemed, to be inside. And the laugh, which she recognized—its depth, its friendliness—normalized the situation to a degree, though for another moment she still wasn't sure what to expect.

"I didn't know if I was gonna make it back. It got dark so fast."

"Are you all right?" she asked, moving toward him but keeping the countertop between them.

"Yeah, I was just walking in the snow and I got a little off track. I usually have a pretty good sense of direction, but I was all turned around. Are you all right? You look stricken."

"Stricken? I was worried. I was about to, I don't know, try to go find help."

"I'm sorry." He took off his hat, coat, gloves, boots. "For making you worry." He went to warm himself by the woodstove. He sounded like someone talking to their over-protective mother, someone burdened by the worry, not appreciative of it. What little she knew about Lila didn't lead Marina to think she was overbearing or overprotective. James wasn't telling Marina that her reaction was out of proportion to what had occurred, but despite apologizing, he wasn't exactly sympathetic to her, he didn't seem to feel any real responsibility for upsetting her. She heard: *Why are you upset when this happened to me?* He was someone who went out alone without a phone. She was not. And then, as if to cheat her of being upset, while giving her no recourse to be upset at being cheated, he was considerate of her, asking her how her afternoon was—that is, at least, before she'd grown concerned.

"It was nice." Not ready to let this all go. Following him to the fire. "But do you know what I really started thinking? It's fucked up but I was wondering if you had, like, a burner phone and you'd gone off to do something I don't want to know about and you'd left me here to . . . I don't even know what."

"A burner phone." He was impressed. "Your writer's imagination." A comment somehow patronizing and gratifying at the same time. He reached for her hand and she moved to warm his still cold fingers between her palms.

He was hungry. Was she hungry? Should they get some dinner going? He was opening cupboards, retrieving what they needed. He apologized again—as if repetition, per-haps, could make up for a lack of conviction—and told her he thought he'd been keeping the pond in sight when he'd headed off the road onto a path in the woods.

She was just glad he was back, safe, she told him.

Later she would wonder which one of them was more self-centered and wonder how much that mattered. He'd told her once that what drew him to his work, on some level, was a desire to become insignificant, to be engaged in something, somewhere that was larger than himself, that wasn't even about him at all. It sounded good, a thoughtful thing to say on an early date. She couldn't let go of a suspicion, though, an intuition, that a desire for negation is still all about oneself.

For now, she watched him set a pot of water on the burner to boil.

The first distance between them had formed. Even the bottle of wine they shared at dinner and after didn't draw them together. His hands on her waist, her hips, none of that tonight. They read their books, they went to sleep. But it occurred to her, lying next to him, that the emergence of that distance was another way of saying they had also developed enough of a closeness that the closeness could be threatened, could be lost.

She left the bar on Rivington alone, a little drunk, somnolent. Heading for the subway home, to let it take her deep underground, tunneling through the East River and surfacing up onto Greenpoint streets that were livelier than those of downtown Manhattan. Younger. Tonight, anyway. And she instinctively took on the contrast as one might take up a banner and wave it in self-definition. Alex Greenman's world was not her world (though she made an exception for Holly). Even James's world was not hers. But this division itself began to feel false, outgrown. So then, what world was hers?

Up the stairs to her apartment, opening the door, going to

wash her summer-dirty feet, the grit from the sidewalk and the subway that had dusted her sandals. Thinking about that woman, Justine, that she'd talked to at the memorial. Justine going home, wherever that might be, with her son. And would her husband be there waiting for her? Partner? Marina was beginning to form a picture of Justine's life. What if it was all a lie, though? (Burner phone life.) What if Justine had simply walked in off the street? An unbalanced individual with no boundaries, who hadn't known James, who didn't have a son, whose name wasn't even Justine. She found the contact in her phone. Justine Mann. She sat on her bed and searched her up. Not all that much, but a few pictures, a professional profile, enough to set Marina's mind at ease. Because she did have a desire to keep talking to Justine. She might just call her after all. She couldn't have said why, exactly, only that it was similar to an impulse she'd had with Holly, at the memorial. Holly had proposed to meet for brunch tomorrow before she left New York and Marina had easily, readily agreed.

"YOU KNOW PEOPLE HATE US," said Alex. He poured more red wine into Holly's glass, sitting across from her at the large dining table. Everyone had gone and it was dark outside, the windows half reflection, half city lights, cars along the Manhattan Bridge. Holly was staying the night, one more night. Their conversation had turned to the guests that had attended the memorial that afternoon, the younger crowd.

"Us who?" Holly asked.

"Boomers. Baby boomers."

"Oh yeah, James had a whole spiel about our generational worthlessness." Though he'd always excluded her and his mother from this. It occurred to her too late, after she spoke, that she and Lila may have escaped James's scorn, but she wasn't sure if Alex had. "Well, they hate successful boomers."

"Simply because we've been successful?"

"Because you've been successful on terms that make success for other people very difficult, not sustainable. You took it all and there's nothing left and you're not aware of that."

"But I am aware of it." Alex had a look, had always had a look, that combined effrontery with guilelessness. And the combination came across as gentle, somehow soft. How could this man truly hurt or offend anyone? Though he had and would continue to. "Every fucking day," he added, "I'm aware of it."

"What do you do about it, though?" Holly's tone was more inquisitive than accusatory, as she drank the wine that Alex brought out, which, of course, was excellent.

"What do you do about it?"

"I don't do anything. They don't hate me. I'm not a success. And I'm technically at the tail end of it. I'm almost between generations. At least, James never hated me."

"You were just born at the wrong time? Into the wrong generation."

"I don't know."

"You're in exile here among us, then."

"How Jewish of you to put it that way," she said. A long-standing joke between them—often enough they would find themselves in situations where she told him she felt like an outsider, a certain unease coupled with a slightly mocking detachment, and he would say: "How Jewish of you."

"How Jewish of *you*." He laughed.

She continued: "I don't have the language for it exactly, I'm sure you know some cultural critics who do, but it's like you bought into it all, even if you bought into it in a creative, sort of bohemian way that didn't look like buying. And to be honest, I'm very happy that you did and that I get to live in exile in your beautiful Manhattan palace for a few days and drink your very excellent wine."

"I'd hardly call it a palace," said Susan, appearing as if out of nowhere, though she'd been sitting at the table the whole time. "And I hardly think we need to apologize to anyone for what we have, what we've worked for."

Holly recalled that Susan had a grown daughter who was something of a disappointment. Holly didn't know the ways in which the daughter fell short. She couldn't even remember the daughter's name offhand. But she found it so much easier and more natural to align with the errant girl than with the critical, let-down mother.

Holly and Susan had earned the same credential—a master's degree in social work—but had accrued such different professional lives. Holly had gone back to school when she could no longer realistically support the belief that dancing, in any of the forms she had pursued, could sustain her. Several years after that point, in truth. Holly had the pragmatism of a defeated dreamer—a "Fine, fuck it" type of pragmatism—and even then, at that seemingly late hour (she was thirty-two), it was social work that she pursued, a field whose moral value so infrequently aligned with its market value. Holly had built up a solid enough private practice as a psychotherapist. Susan, though, had managed a more profitable trajectory over the years, cultivating an affluent clientele in New York City who could afford to pay her not insignificant rates even without insurance.

"You shouldn't apologize for what you've worked for, but you shouldn't forget what you've been given," said Holly. "What you've taken. Sorry, what *we've* taken, generationally speaking."

"Well then, to taking!" said Alex, raising his glass, clinking it with Susan's. And to the extent that Holly couldn't tell how sardonic he was being, she understood why it worked with him and Susan and why it had never worked, not really, between the two of them.

It wasn't quite exile, being there, with them. It was more like displacement from your own past, and therefore from your present and your future. Disorientation in the sense of not being sure which direction you were facing and what any direction would necessarily even mean. It was a suspension, too, of reality—of daily life, at least. She wasn't sure how much of this was due to being here with Alex and Susan in Alex's old apartment and how much was because James was gone. James and Lila, both. The suspension of reality, of time, wasn't terrible. It didn't hurt. When reality and time resumed it would hurt. She was drunk. She didn't drink much anymore and now she was on her third glass of wine. She would have a dense, short block of deep sleep in a strange bed with strange dreams and then wake up early and unwell. Susan will bring me tea on a nice tray, Holly thought. And I'll say thank you, Susan, this is lovely. I'll ask her, not so innocently, what's the deal with your daughter? And Susan the therapist will excuse me; it's the grief talking.

She was drunk enough, loose enough, to ask a favor of Alex. James didn't have much property, having moved out of the place he'd shared with Marina. He'd put his belongings in a small storage locker to sort through when he returned to America. Now it would be Holly's job to do the sorting. He did, though, have a cache of expensive photographic paraphernalia, including the camera and memory cards he'd been traveling with, salvaged from the wreck that killed him. Those, too, belonged to Holly now. Returned to her with her nephew's body. She wasn't sure if the memory cards had been damaged but she hadn't wanted to risk damaging them further, handling them improperly because she didn't know any better. But Alex would know better.

"Could we look at them?" she asked. "You've got the right equipment?"

"Probably," he said. "But are you sure you want to do this? Now?"

"No, I'm not sure. But I may never be. If not now, when?"

She didn't know whom she was quoting, but she knew that it was a Jewish expression, and he didn't have to say it—*How Jewish of you*—he simply smiled.

"Can I bring my wine?"

"Yes, if you're careful."

"I'm always careful." She didn't know what she even meant by that. It wasn't true. But the effect was flirtatious and, in Susan's presence, claim-staking. When she went to retrieve the memory cards from her bag, in the guest room, she imagined the look Susan gave Alex, the look they gave each other when she was out of sight: coupled and collusive.

She followed Alex down a set of stairs to an area she'd never seen because it hadn't been part of the place originally. He and Susan had recently annexed some of the floor below and this white-walled, well-organized space had become his office. Susan hadn't come with them. She was where? Giving them space? Preserving her own space?

They sat by a monitor and Alex opened up a screen of images. Sites of "environmental trauma" was how James's latest work had been described to Holly. From what she understood, for this last assignment, James had been commissioned by a nonprofit to document a part of Western Africa where they could no longer grow crops because of climate change. Mali. Niger. The rains there were unpredictable, the soil now bone dry. To avoid starvation, people tried to head across the Sahara, north for Libya, Algeria, maybe even Europe. The nonprofit had a reporter, a journalist, a writer, whatever you called it—a word person. They needed a picture person.

Going through the files, she let Alex set the pace, because he knew better, and he made noises like *hmm* and *nnh* before clicking to enlarge the next image. Alex's murmuring and her silence in contrast made her wonder if she hadn't seen too many photographs in her life, particularly of horror, so many that they started to look alike, they didn't shock her into feeling or action, let alone murmuring. They no longer horrified. You turned the page, scrolled on. Image fatigue. What captivated her wasn't the straight depiction of suffering or disaster. It was the human rendered strange in the world. Sometimes it was the absence of human form, the disappearance of it. A photograph of a used face mask, its thin stretchy straps soiled with grime, lying on shiny green tile. The detritus, the evidence, of a dying city.

Even these pictures failed to move her in the way she wanted to be moved. Though in some way James was in every shot—they were seeing what he saw and how he saw it—she didn't feel closeness to him, only its absence, and disappointment in herself. Alcohol is a depressant, she reminded herself, as she reached for her glass.

Alex saw differently than she did. He talked about getting the photos in front of a certain editor, unless they needed to go to the organization that James had been shooting for. Which they probably did. And there must have been notes, somewhere, of what exactly each image was, no? They'd have to sort it out, but in any case, it was really good work and it should be seen. His praise and enthusiasm stirred a vicarious, sentimental pride in her that almost—almost—counteracted her alienation.

James, little James, his little shoulders by the fogged-up window of her old car, drawing cat whiskers.

"I think it's important that he leave some sort of legacy," said Alex.

"Yes, of course," she replied. Though it sounded like a lot to do. What did leaving a legacy even involve? Alex didn't elaborate. What Holly was more interested in glimpsing was the impossible: all that James never captured, all his thoughts, his half-thoughts, his memories, the flashes of him—all of it, just gone now, and no one would ever know. The unknowable legacy that everyone has and that disappears completely with them.

"I'm really tired all of a sudden," she said.

"It's been a long day."

"I'm gonna head up. You coming?"

"In a bit," he said. It was late but he was newly energized, in his element, in this workspace of his that had nothing to do with any memory Holly had of him—any association other than this present emptiness.

Susan had gone to bed. They still slept next to each other, Susan and Alex, in the same bed, or at least they had for the nights Holly had stayed there. Why did that surprise her? Why had she imagined a sexless, separate-bed existence for the two of them? That they would have been driven apart by certain night habits, snoring. Why had she wanted that for them?

In the guest room, she took off the dark clothes she'd had on all day and changed into the t-shirt she wore to bed. The covers were so soft, so nicely weighted. What more did she want from her hosts? They'd given her what they could. In the darkness of the room, a line of light at the bottom of the window shade, a curtain seemed to fall on her resentment of Susan and Alex, as if the resentment were no longer onstage, as if there were no stage, only heavy eyes, and sleep.

Susan did not come to her with tea in the morning. Susan had likely gone to work or—it was Saturday—shopping, maybe to her gym. Something to take her out of the loft. It was past ten. Holly, who'd slept soundly and then tossed and turned, and then slept again, found a glass of water in the kitchen, downed a couple of pain relievers for her head, and then, on her way back to the guest room to get dressed for the day, encountered Alex in the hall. She wasn't wearing any pants.

An old reflex, his eyes took her in. And then a new reflex: he averted his gaze.

Her legs no longer looked like they once did, she knew this. She was no longer that young woman, naked by the window, the woman in the photograph. But he was no longer that young man. What did he expect? What did she expect? They moved around each other, shuffling glances, understanding half laughs.

"Why do you have those on?" she said, pointing to his chinos.

"Habit," he said. "Convention. My God, what have I become?"

"Good question, something to think about," she said, slipping into the guest room and closing the door.

She could still be quick with him. Even, or especially, in her embarrassment. Even waiting for the pain relievers to kick in. Her legs couldn't possibly be any less attractive than Susan's. She still had the long-limbed proportions of a dancer, though not the muscle tone. But the tiny purple veins along her thighs, at her knees and her ankles, reminded her of marble, or of a wall of rock once created by a flowing river whose waters have leveled off. On a good day, at least. In the right light. But . . . they were her legs! How wonderful they had been and how wonderful they still were, even if they couldn't leap or jump the way they used to. Fuck you, Alex, she thought. Fuck a whole lot of things.

Still without pants, she raised the window shade to a view of rooftops and water towers, wispy clouds against the blue sky. This unmooring in her—it was some disappointment that Alex hadn't asked her if she would take off the rest of her clothes and go stand in the sun, and some disappointment in herself for having wanted that. Disappointment in her own disappointment. It would have been an exercise in nostalgia, and those never go well. Before she could conclude, though, that she would have said yes and done it, if only he'd asked (why didn't he ask?), a text from Marina came through on her phone. *Running a little late. Leaving soon.* There wasn't time, besides. The plan they'd made the day before: brunch with Alex before she headed back home. Marina had been invited along at some point during the memorial.

Alex kept his hands in his pockets the whole way and she was quiet on the walk with him to the restaurant he'd suggested, not far from his home, where he knew the staff. And they knew him—the celebrated photographer—even the younger staffers, who likely didn't care who he was but had at least been told to google him and pretend. It was a place that served plenty of New York–famous types. New York–famous types frequented it for that reason—no gawking, just enough flattery. A bright, airy atmosphere, convivial but not too loud to talk. Tables were filling up, but the room wasn't overcrowded. Marina hadn't yet arrived.

Alex was all benevolence—*After you*—and though she had long appreciated his chivalry, the slightly smug show of it annoyed her now. It would have made her spiky if her body hadn't felt weak, her skin papery. How good it was to sit.

"You okay?" he asked.

"I'm fine. I probably just need some coffee."

"The coffee's good here," he said, and pointed to an item on the menu, something that sounded like a delicious version of a simple dish. "Humble" was a word she'd heard but never used in relation to food. She imagined it got thrown around in reviews of this establishment.

"Would you say it's humble?" she asked.

"I would say . . . they know what they're doing here." In the pause between what he would say and what he said, she heard his rising irritation with her. After all, here he was, only being kind, doing something nice for her, and she was meeting him with mockery.

"Well, I'm glad someone does." She eased off. "I need that. I'm not sure I know what I'm doing."

"Holly."

"I'm fine. Really."

"Let's get you that coffee." He made a subtle hand movement and soon enough a woman around Marina's age in a spiffy black apron appeared with a silver coffee pot. Holly thought of the brown-bronze coffee pot, the plate of pancakes and scuffed flatware, the lantern of rippled amber glass hanging over the table—a photograph Alex had taken so many years ago, part of an early series that had garnered him attention. Flat, affectless, mundane, American.

He's navigated the world better than she has, hasn't he? With his subtle hand movements. He is New York famous. She could have maybe been New York famous, too, once. Maybe. There was a point there when it had seemed ever so briefly possible . . . and then there was no longer a point.

Marina came in like a breeze, Holly thought, grateful for her presence, a third person in the dynamic. Younger, refreshing. Alex, too, seemed lightened, happy to have someone besides Holly here. Someone who wasn't Susan, because of course that didn't make it any easier with Holly. For a couple of days, around his wife, an exclusionary intimacy had existed between him and Holly. And then—a timer going off—the intimacy, or at the least the exclusiveness of it, had vanished. When had the timer sounded? Last night? Had he seen something in James's pictures, in their very quality, that made him a little cagey and tentative around her now? Or had he found her lacking because she couldn't look at those images with any rigor or distance? Or was it this morning? When he saw her without her pants and almost immediately looked away?

She and Alex both made a quasi-parental show of welcoming Marina, asking how she was, how her night was. Marina played the filial role easily enough. She looked a little tired— Holly wondered how she'd spent her night. A loose shirt, jeans. Hair swept up messily, nothing on her face except the black cat's-eye liner she wore. Her youth, Holly thought. I could never get a cat's eye right, I could only do stage makeup, and now my eyelids sag too much for it anyway.

But with Marina's arrival, too, came a sense of anti-climax. The hotel brunch, say, after a wedding, for the out-of-towners, the stragglers who hadn't the good sense to have already left. That inkling that you've stayed too long and that life is being lived better elsewhere.

What did they all have to say to each other that they hadn't said over the course of the last couple of days?

As another server came to take their order and fill their water glasses, nothing sounded quite right to Holly and her fluttering stomach. She requested the most humble-looking item involving toast that she could find on the menu. Alex ordered his "usual" and Marina asked for a dish that prompted the server to call her selection an "excellent choice."

Alex and Marina began talking politely to each other, while Holly tried to look as if she were listening even though she wasn't entirely hearing or comprehending what they were saying. Her ears weren't working right. She saw them laughing mildly and joined in. But the sound she made was less a laugh than a high-pitched mewl, part of it escaped and the rest curdled in her throat. She reached for her water, her hand shaking, and she dropped the glass, recoiling as it shattered on the floor.

Heads turned, two waiters came over to clean up the mess, and Holly saw Alex's face contract.

"I'm so sorry," she said. Her hand continued trembling and she was crying so that even as she wiped the tears the away, they returned. "I'm so sorry. Is everyone okay?"

"It's just water," said Marina, kindly.

She took Holly's hand and held it still in her own. Alex, by contrast, didn't know what to do for her or for himself, beyond barely concealing his shame. She'd been so calm, she'd kept it together, the whole time she'd been there in New York and now, just before it had come to an end, she had embarrassed him. With her loose, pale legs. Her lack of aesthetic appreciation for James's work, her lack of understanding the social value implicit in that appreciation. Her clumsy fingers.

The heads turned away, conversation picked up again at nearby tables, and Alex, to redirect the three of them, told Marina about the work they found on James's memory cards. How she should really see it. Holly was listening but mostly she was trying to focus her gaze on something to normalize her breath and stop herself sobbing, stop herself from embarrassing Alex any further. It had become about that—sparing him. How had it become about that? Her problem, not his. And did her habitual acceptance of this—her tendency toward conciliation and amelioration over anger, at least when it came to Alex Greenman—have something to do with the reality that Alex had attained a certain status in the world and she had not?

Out the window, along a city sidewalk, a pigeon alighted on a drab green mailbox, a postal relay box, and the bird's wings and claws, its ticking head, made Holly think about her sister. Of a time when Lila had been in the hospital, before it was clear she was, in fact, dying, and she and James were down in the gift shop looking, with questions, at a stuffed satin cat (Why satin? Wasn't that a sort of "sexy" material and therefore "adult"? Wasn't its expression more come hither than cute? Or was the expression more indifferent than anything? A little haughty, long and slim and downward-looking. What sort of kid do you buy that for? What type of adult? They decided to get it for Lila, decided they *had* to get it for Lila) when a bird flew in through the automatic doors of the hospital lobby. The bird, its flight and entrapment, reminded Holly of a poem she loved: a father watching his young daughter writing a story up in her room and the father thinking back, about a bird, a starling, that had been trapped in his daughter's room and finally, after failed and injurious attempts, had escaped out the window, into the linden trees, and what the father, the poet, wished for his writer-daughter, wished so hard and so deeply for her. How he'd forgotten that it was always, the poet said, a matter of life and death.

The pigeon flew from the mailbox. Holly was still crying, in intervals, when the food arrived. It would stop for a moment and then return. She would need another white napkin soon to replace the one in her hands, too wet and smeared with mascara.

"Holly?" said Marina. "I think we should go. Just maybe go for a walk, get some air."

Holly nodded, acquiescent.

"Alex?" said Marina, almost as if she had to snap to get his attention.

"You go," he replied, preoccupied. "I'll settle up here."

He gave Marina the keys to his place and said he would meet them back there soon.

Holly was unsteady as she stood, leaning on Marina a little as they left the restaurant, but she made it out to the sidewalk without collapsing, without breaking anything else.

"I'm sorry, Marina."

"You have nothing to be sorry for."

"You came all the way here."

Marina shrugged.

"It just, it all hit me in a way it hasn't before."

"Of course. I kind of couldn't believe how smoothly you'd handled everything. Been handling everything."

"It helps me, taking care of things, being useful. Gives me some measure of control. Or a semblance of it. And then it all crumbles. In a nice public place. You can't take me anywhere. Anymore. And shit, look at this—" she held up the damp, soiled napkin she'd taken with her unthinkingly. A flag of halfhearted surrender. Her face was still wet.

"Here," said Marina, taking the napkin and stuffing it in her own bag to dispose of later. And though they could have walked, just as she and Alex had walked here, Marina hailed a taxi and rode with Holly back to the Greenmans'. She went up with Holly in the elevator, walked her through the front space, to a living area, and sat her down on the couch. How competent this young woman was. Though Holly remembered how out of sorts Marina had been on the phone, that day she'd called to tell Holly that James was dead. Maybe this is what they did and would do for each other, alternate as ballasts.

"This place looks so different today," said Marina. "Without anybody here."

Emptied of people, and perhaps as Holly now saw it through Marina's eyes, the loft invited trespass. The well-stocked kitchen, copper pots on open shelves, apricots in a wooden bowl, a loaf of bread wrapped in paper on the butcher-block counter.

"I'm hungry," Marina said.

"I'm sorry, you didn't get to eat."

"No, I didn't mean it like that, to blame you. You must be hungry, too." Marina pulled a good knife from a magnetic strip and cut into the bread, not without a certain vengeance. She found an expensive looking jar of jam in a cupboard, and made toast for the two of them, and tea, bringing it to Holly on a tray. The dirty cutlery she left in the sink, unwashed. And she would leave this tray out, too, along with their crumb-strewn plates.

Holly had stopped crying—weeping, really—and her breath had steadied itself. She'd never wept like that, almost unceasing, sprung from a source inside of her that she couldn't regulate. She hadn't wept like that when either of her parents had died, when Lila had died, or when she'd gotten the news about James.

It was never very bright in Alex's loft; even when the sun came in, it shone at an angle, diffused. People looked good in this light. Marina looked good. As if this place belonged to her—or should. Fuck that guy, Marina's gestures all said, with more delight than anger. Let's eat his fucking food and lie all over his furniture. And Holly wanted to say "Okay, I get it, but don't you think . . ." Think what? Marina moved about with a freedom Holly couldn't resist. Even as Marina's blunt anger struck Holly as a little too accusatory, of Alex, of her. Correct, but accusatory: What's wrong with you, Holly? Why are you so quick and so cowardly in your forgiveness? Marina's anger also struck Holly as a little young. The anger of a woman for whom there was a right and wrong, black and white and no gray, and who was only beginning to know what it was like to lose people, over time. Who likely had no strong sense of the constriction that occurred, the narrowing of circles, over time. When Holly had been Marina's age, did she have Marina's feelings? She and Alex were on-again, off-again by that point, though mostly they had settled into a solid friendship. And then he had met and married a woman named Thea. They divorced about as quickly as they'd wed. Holly hadn't exactly expected the split to clear the way for something else, something new between her and Alex, but when he'd gone and married Susan, she'd experienced the news as a kind of dulled revelation. *Oh.*

Possibly the difference between Holly's reaction to Alex at the restaurant and the way Marina saw it was due to a generational shift—for the better?—in outlook. A lower tolerance for certain (male?) behavior. But Holly bristled at the idea that she was a coward.

"Look, I don't know Alex all that well," Marina said. "But."

"Yeah." Holly sighed, instinctively about to apologize for him—to offer a banal reminder that everyone deals with these things differently—before she stopped herself. Marina didn't want or need to hear that. Marina wanted Holly to agree, and since she couldn't, not with the vehemence Marina required, Holly decided to take a different tack.

"I'm sorry it didn't work out with you and James," Holly said.

"Me too," said Marina. She crunched a piece of toast, let the crumbs fall on the couch. Marina hesitated. She tried to offer an explanation to Holly. That her relationship with James had had a weight, but not a propulsion, a forward movement. And she hadn't always believed it needed that. But time began to impose itself—certain things would cease to be hovering possibilities and would either happen or not happen. A commitment? A family, even, maybe? That all of it was still conceptual enough for James had probably drawn them together at the beginning, until it started to draw them apart.

"I don't know if I can say this to you," said Marina. "Or if I should."

"Say it."

"It's just strange. With James, you know, we ended things, and so there's an assumption that we'd be out of each other's lives anyway."

"It's not always that clean, though. It rarely is."

"No, I know. But what I mean is, I expected to have to mourn, in a way. Mourn what it was that we had."

"But not like this."

"Right. And now it's like he's in my life in this whole different way."

Holly wondered if Marina knew or understood what she was thinking: that there is a kind of person who is never out of your life. Or put another way, there is a kind of person for whom other people rarely disappear completely. Just look at where they were, in the home of her former lover, from so very long ago. Holly wasn't yet sure if Marina was that kind of person.

"I'm going to go to Vermont, to scatter his ashes," said Holly. "You could come, if you'd like to."

"That's what he wanted?" asked Marina. "See, I never knew that. I didn't know things like that about him. Vermont?"

"There's a place up there he used to go with his mother."

"Oh," said Marina, with some relief. "Well, that I knew. I knew about that place. When are you going?"

"I thought I might wait until winter. For the snow."

"Thank you. For even suggesting it," Marina answered. "Can I think about it?"

Holly understood Marina's reluctance or thought she did. But what if she were to put it to Marina this way: Would you come with me? For my sake?

She knew what Marina meant, of course she did, about James now being in her life in a new, ongoing way. How his absence, his ghost, predicated new circumstances. If James had made it to the airport, boarded the plane, and flown back from Germany as planned, Holly in all likelihood would never have seen Marina again. Now she didn't quite know how to leave her.

"There's time. I'm not in a rush. Think about it and let me know."

"I will." Marina eyed the tea and toast that Holly had barely touched. "Are you going to be all right? To catch your train, later? Maybe you should reschedule for tomorrow or something."

Holly waved away Marina's concern, she would be fine.

"I have to get back. I have clients on the calendar."

"I'm sure they'd understand."

"You've never been in therapy." A question and a statement.

"No," said Marina. "Well, not yet. Should I be?"

Holly gave Marina her "therapist smile"—suggestive and elusive. And then, to continue in that suggestive and elusive vein, she said to Marina: "Are you writing much?"

"No. Not lately. But you know, I remember meeting Alex Greenman with James once, it must have been a couple of years ago, and he asked me what I did, and I said I worked in communications. And Alex nodded—bored—and James piped in and was like, 'She won't tell you but she's a writer.' And I was irritated and embarrassed and grateful all at the same time. But I don't even know . . . are you a writer if you don't have any readers?"

"If a tree falls in the forest, yeah, it falls. Someone's going to find the tree and see. Eventually."

"Find it decomposing."

Marina clearly had her defenses.

"Well, I would read your work. If you would ever want that."

Encouragement was no small thing. Sometimes, Holly remembered, it was all you had. It was a terrible myth— the notion that you could toil in obscurity, in a complete vacuum—and produce a body of work that had any resonance and meaning. You needed to find your audience. You needed peers, you needed conversation and community, if not for support then at least to push against.

"You're very kind, Holly."

They fell into a silence in which Holly watched Marina truly consider her offer, her interest. No more than a moment, though.

"What do you think is keeping Alex?" Marina asked. "Shouldn't he be back by now?"

She seemed disappointed, as if she'd wanted Alex to ring or knock, to have him wait out in the hall until they opened the door, and then to see them there taking advantage of his hospitality, sprawling all over it.

"I wonder if he isn't down on the sidewalk," said Holly. "Waiting to see you go before he comes up. I can't imagine he's particularly proud of himself."

"I actually should get going soon," said Marina. "If you'll really be okay?"

Holly assured Marina she'd be fine, and they embraced. Then the young woman was gone. And when she was alone, in the absence of anyone else, the loft was no longer an old friend, or a familiar phantom from her past, or even a site to vandalize, as Marina might have wanted. It was only a place where Holly didn't belong.

In the guest room, she collected her things into her roller bag. It was possible that Alex wouldn't return before she needed to head for Penn Station. She had the key. How would he get in? He'd have a spare somewhere. Or he'd meet up with Susan, get a key from her. They weren't entirely two separate people, Susan and Alex. He'd say to himself: *Susan, Susan, thank God for you, Susan.* And Susan would later find all the vengeful crumbs on the couch, maybe a greasy fingerprint on the pillow upholstery, and on the table the cold tea bags, like soft, discarded organs from a small creature. Susan would clear them away before Alex even noticed them, before he even had a chance to wonder where they came from.

Holly heard the buzzer.

In the doorway, she noticed how Alex's jacket hung off his rounded shoulders, which had escaped her before. The type of twill jacket he'd been wearing since she'd first known him and that once gave him exactly the look he was going for: offhand and unpretentious but attending to detail. Now she saw, for the first time, that his face and his body were both looser and bonier. What had kept her from seeing this change? She hadn't wanted to see it, as he hadn't wanted to see her legs. The jacket was cut for a different man, a younger man. He must have known this, and yet he still wore it. And he stooped, even, there in the doorway, apologizing. She accepted his apology, but that didn't alleviate the feeling that he'd failed her. When she let him take her bag out to the sidewalk for her, the gesture was too little and too late. And when he hugged her goodbye, he maintained a distance, he didn't fully pull her to him, and she could feel an imaginary Susan between them. She wanted to displace his reaction onto his wife, blame it on Susan's influence, but it wasn't working. Imaginary Susan slipped away and it was only Alex hugging her. Nothing between them, not Susan, not a camera, nothing at all except stale air rising off the sidewalk.

IN AN ODD WAY, Marina was grateful to Alex Greenman, for honing her generalized, roving anger, giving it a specific target. She swept herself up the street, savage, from Greenman's loft, along the Bowery, to Nolita, one of those neighborhood names that had come into parlance when she was a child.

She hadn't walked off her irritability when she passed the window display of a bookstore. *Don't look, don't fucking look.* She looked. She even stopped, seeing a poster publicizing an event with a writer she'd gone to school with. A woman named Dahlia, with whom she was friendly enough, whose success Marina wanted to be big enough to support and applaud. *Don't begrudge.* She begrudged.

Dahlia. Fucking Dahlia! It wasn't even that Marina wanted to write like Dahlia. (Though she wouldn't have minded a smartly designed, prominently displayed poster in a bookstore window.) No, not at all like Dahlia.

Why don't you write much anymore? James would ask. *You're a writer. You should write!* He meant to encourage her, she knew, to embolden her, not to scold. But he didn't understand how it worked—how it worked for her. As if it were that easy. If you wanted something, as James saw it, you fought for it.

But James, have you never sustained a knockout blow, the kind that makes you lose your fighting spirit?

Knockouts, yeah. But eventually you get up.

I don't know. Maybe I get up and then exit the ring. Maybe I take off my gloves. I don't know enough about boxing to keep this metaphor going.

I just don't think you should give up.

His belief in her would make her stomach quiver and a warmth would rush to her head.

Dahlia now looked out at her from the poster in the window, intense come-into-my-lair eyes to go with her intense, come-into-my-lair thoughts, no doubt.

Fucking Dahlia. Marina stormed on. Stormed inwardly, at least. *You shouldn't have looked at that window display.*

But you did. James's voice entered her head. *So now what?*

So now, I want to talk shit about her to you in ghost form. Can we do that?

We can do that. We can definitely do that. If you want. But what if you went to this event?

Why? Why on earth would I do that?

What if you could be open to that?

If I could be open to that . . . She couldn't complete the sentence, couldn't find a "then" to the "if."

I don't mean in a transactional way, James said. *I mean in a receptive way.*

Receptive? I don't know. Is that how you felt about your peers? Or about Alex Greenman? Open? I guess so, because it never seemed like his acclaim made you insecure or bitter. It never seemed like his acclaim had much of an effect on you either way.

I'd be lying if I said it didn't. But contempt only gets you so far, Marina.

But James, I have so much of it! Maybe it could get me far enough!

How she wished she could turn around and see him now. See him smiling at her. That he would be there and put his arm around her and they'd keep on walking together down the block.

But his voice disappeared and she was alone again, walking down the block by herself and down into the station, waiting for the train. On the platform she took out her phone.

This is Marina, she texted. *From the memorial service . . .*

Oh, hi! Came an immediate reply from Justine. Overeager? Or simply considerate? Simply . . . there?

Wondering if you'd want to get together soon?

Justine suggested times and places with a swiftness and grammar that struck Marina as parental, caretaking, and Marina welcomed it, this setting in motion of something new, as she stepped into the subway car.

THE REAL ESTATE AGENT had been an actress once, years ago. In theater and on a daytime soap when soap operas still filmed in New York. It wasn't, she said to Justine, that tough a transition, professionally. Being a performer was a plus when you had to show people apartments. But this apartment, she said, didn't require her to fake it. It was just that good. Trust me, you'll see, leading her into a small lobby with a short flight of worn stone stairs. In a long mirror, oxidized with age, Justine could see herself seeing the agent, whose nostrils flared as she pulled back a sliding metal door, thick with beige paint. She led Justine into this elevator, made to accommodate no more than four people comfortably. Paneled in dark wood. Up they went to the fifth floor, the top. Two apartments per floor.

"So, what happened to Adam?" the agent asked. "He got hung up?"

"He has to work late, but I didn't want to cancel."

The agent arranged her face into a look, what she must have done in scenes where the direction called for a knowing, conspiratorial half-smile. But Justine wasn't sure what the conspiracy was here, what they were both in on together. Until the agent opened a door directly from the elevator into the apartment itself. A living room with such high ceilings, such fine moldings, a working fireplace. Justine had never seen anything like it in New York, this particular quality of shadowy, faded grandeur. Heavy green-gold curtains running the length of the wall rendered the otherwise empty room stage-like and the powder blue walls and powder blue carpet added an aqueous quality, enclosing, a womb.

"Let's shed a little light on the subject," said the agent, opening the curtains and revealing two tall windows, full green branches of trees and the slate-shingled roof of the apartment building across the street. How quiet it was, not more than a few blocks from the elevated tracks of the 7 train over the clatter and rumble of Roosevelt Avenue.

And still the room was dusky, as the last of the day's sun came in. It had been cleared of any furniture. A couple of marks on the carpet indicated where there might have been a floral patterned couch or a chair, and though it didn't smell of smoke, Justine saw quite clearly a side table off toward the corner, a pack of cigarettes lying on it. And she saw the ghost of the woman who smoked them: she was thin, she wore a trim polyester shirt tucked into a knee length skirt, low heels, a dark gray bob brushed up and away from her face. A skeptical, narrow face, a little beaky, a little mean.

The agent said: "Some new paint, of course, and you'd want to pull up the carpet. But I mean! Right?"

The ghost of the woman said: "Do you know how long I saved to buy this carpet?" She exhaled, tapped her cigarette into a glass ashtray.

The agent said: "Gorgeous wood floors, see? Gorgeous." And she directed Justine down a little uncarpeted hall that led to the bedroom on one side and a bathroom on the other. Glass transoms above the doors.

There wasn't much of the woman in the bedroom, which had also been emptied and hastily whitewashed, but she appeared again in the bathroom, with its pink and black tile, the pink sink and toilet. She sat on the edge of the pink tub, beneath a bare shower curtain rod. The scent of various ointments. A small, frosted window painted shut but which let in a glazed light.

"Grandma smell, I know," said the agent.

"Christ," said the woman.

"You'll open the window, air it out. It's charming in a retro way," said the agent. "Or maybe it's a gut. I'd gut it, if it were me. Start fresh. Maybe more neutral?"

"*You*," said the woman, taking a drag. "The pink made me happy."

"In any case, it's a good size," said the agent. "And, oh, the water pressure's great." She turned the taps to demonstrate. The woman, who had rematerialized by the door, stared mutely at the running water.

The galley kitchen had been updated around the time of the pink bathroom.

Thin maple cabinets, hardware that looked to be from the 1950s, maybe the early 1960s. Outdated appliances, no dishwasher. A dumbwaiter that people use mostly for cable wires now, said the agent. Even, on the wall, a yellow rotary phone.

"It's got a lot of potential," said the agent.

Out of the kitchen window, the fire escape led up to the roof and down to a garden courtyard.

"Does this open?" Justine asked, of the security gate that barred the window.

"I'm sure it does," said the agent.

"Oh, it does," said the woman. "I had it installed after a third break-in. But that was years ago. And I hated to do it. That was my spot, out there. In the summer, especially. My neighbor Dorothy lived in the apartment next door, which is the same, just flipped around, and we would crawl out of our kitchens, with our cigarettes, and sit and talk. Dorothy didn't look mean, or hard, not like me, she was all softness, roundness, but God, she was wicked. I never laughed so hard."

"Does Dorothy still live there?" Justine asked the woman.

"Oh, no, Dorothy's long gone. The women live there now."

"The women?"

"A couple of middle-aged lesbians."

Justine couldn't tell if this was simply a statement of fact or if there was an undertone. Acerbic, bigoted.

"Do you like them?" she asked.

"They get things done," said the woman. "They're efficient."

The woman shrugged.

Off the kitchen was the dining room—"You could take out the wall, if you wanted, I've seen that done," said the agent—and the dining room had French doors that led to what the agent called a sunroom, which most people in these buildings used as a second bedroom.

This room, which had also been painted white, down to the radiator cover, like the proper bedroom, didn't contain the woman either. It was like an aerie or some quiet spot high up in a castle. Walls of long windows that looked out and over into their mirror image in a twin brick building across a lawn, spanning the length of a block, in half canopy under tall elms.

A door to what Justine assumed was a closet turned out to be another bathroom, which she couldn't quite get over. Two bathrooms, in a New York City apartment, that could potentially be hers! This one was smaller, and it seemed it had never been redone, still the same as when this building had been constructed, top of the line in the 1920s. Well-appointed places for well-appointed people on what had been farmland in Queens. Jackson Heights. There had been a golf course across the street; then the stock market crashed and for decades after you could get these places for a song. Only now were they significantly rising in value. Two varieties were currently turning over: the apartments inhabited and untouched for years by elderly people, and those that had more recently already been in the hands of first-wave gentrifiers: the childless middle-aged lesbians, or younger couples, who eventually had more than one child and moved to New Jersey.

Justine would be part of a second wave, and the plan was to find an apartment with two bedrooms, one of which could be for a child. She was, then, almost three months pregnant. Her first-ever first trimester. It was a strange time she was in, of being detail-oriented and on top of everything— appointments, guidebooks, learning what she should and shouldn't do—and simultaneously giving herself over to the unknown. A surrender of herself, an offering, to whatever was to come.

Whatever was to come: if it involved living in such an apartment in New York, it would require that she return to her corporate cocoon as soon as she could after her maternity leave. And the unknown: if the future was uncharted, it was also narrower now. It foreclosed on an old idea she had of herself: the young woman who hadn't minded living in a filthy, rotting room and using a fungal bathroom because the filthiness, the rot, and the mold meant her priorities were in the right place. That young woman who had once gone walking with a young man who had matched her, or so she'd thought, in artistic ambition. What had happened to that young woman? Had the young man merely surpassed her or had she languished and shrunk? Both? She never did apply to grad school; she'd been too busy, too satisfied with the steady, incremental affirmation, in the form of pay and status and respect, that her day job provided, a day job which had become a career—nothing to take for granted. Only recently had her decisions started to haunt her.

"Who's the seller?" Justine asked the agent. "What's her name?"

"Her?" said the agent.

"I mean . . . their, or whatever, whoever. I'm just curious."

"It's an estate, I think," said the agent. "The adult children."

Adult children. It struck Justine as an oxymoron that should have had resonance for her, now that she was, ostensibly, an adult, soon to have a child.

"They were always more adult than I ever was," said the woman.

"But you raised them," said Justine.

"If you asked them, they would probably say, *She was here.* That we were in the same place at the same time. That they raised themselves despite me. My husband, their father, died young. He was the kind one and then he was gone, and they had me to contend with."

The woman wandered away from the French doors, through the dining area to the powder blue living room, the womb of carpet and curtains.

"So!" said the agent. "Look around, let me know what you think. I can get you in again if you're serious about it and your husband wants to see."

"Great, thanks," said Justine.

Adam should see this place, she thought, looking out the windows of the sunroom. If we paint the whole thing white, she wondered, does the woman disappear? Should I want her to go? What if we pulled up the powder blue carpet and put a new color on those living room walls? Pulled down the heavy gold curtains? It seemed wrong to do that. A desecration.

"Well, that's a bit much," said the woman, returning, by the mantle of the fireplace. "Desecration! It's musty and worn. It needs to be refreshed. And you should want me to go. I want me to go."

They took up the linoleum in the kitchen, but the pink and black bathroom tile, what they could salvage, remained. They had the green-gold curtains cleaned and rehung, considered new powder blue carpeting, but pulled it up and refinished the floors beneath instead. Justine never got the name of the woman who had lived there, but in her head it was Eileen. Or Irene. She hadn't come back, hadn't spoken to Justine since that first viewing with the agent. But they, she and Adam, would channel her now and then. Adam, who'd never encountered her ghost, and was only going on the description offered by Justine, sounded vaguely like Katharine Hepburn when he did it. It was nonsense: "Goin' out for a pack a smokes," he'd say, before running an errand. Or "Who told you you could take a break?" when Justine was sitting on the couch. "Calm down. Where's the fire?" Justine would say when he would knock on the bathroom door before work— "You can wait your turn"—before letting him in. They now lived in what they'd been told was the most diverse neighborhood in the most diverse borough in New York City; they imagined it bred in Eileen/Irene a grudging tolerance that she believed entitled her to make the occasional racist or ethnically derogative comment. They didn't imitate these, but Justine recognized the spiritual residue of Eileen/Irene in the snippets of conversation she occasionally overheard among old people on benches when she brought Oliver to the one park in the neighborhood.

She would meet up with Kat, another new mother, at the park, and they would talk as they pushed their children on the baby swings. Kat had grown up in Brooklyn, had a PhD in art history, and lived two blocks away. Her father was white, her mother was Black. Eileen/Irene—Kat said she knew the type. Her father's mother. Her grandmother had owned the apartment where Kat and Kat's wife now lived, had left it to her when she died. As a child, Kat would go with her father to visit her grandmother. Mostly what Kat remembered on these visits was the dish of Andes candies wrapped in their green foil, always set out on the coffee table. The gilt-framed print of flowers on the wall. A family of ceramic cats in a bookcase. Bud vases of hobnail milk glass. The sort of stuff you'd now find at thrift stores. An aesthetic that would later, when she thought about it as an adult—when she better understood how uncomfortable her grandmother had been with Kat's father's interracial marriage—strike Kat as complacent. Unapologetic, unashamed of its complacency.

Kat and her wife, Laura, hadn't gutted the place, but they came close. (Laura—Justine saw so little of her, the breadwinner, working long hours at a management consulting job nobody quite understood; not even Kat, it seemed. "Laura sees it like a series of big puzzles," Kat had once said, and then trailed off.)

"There's no way we weren't moving in," Kat had said. "No way we'd pass it up. But I had to, you know, cleanse the place."

"Should we have gotten rid of the gold curtains Eileen left?" Justine had asked.

"You ask that like they're a Confederate monument or something."

"Well, are they? In a way? Curtains of white supremacy?"

Kat looked like she was pretending to look like she didn't have the patience.

"I'm only ever going to see curtains of white supremacy now when I come over." She laughed. Still, the conversation hung about Justine, left her sitting with her own complacency, long after they'd gotten up from the bench and taken their children home.

That was over two years ago. Now, on Fridays in the summer, in the early evening after work, the young parents—the young mothers mostly—got together in a run of enclosed green space the length of a city block just beyond the more formal garden courtyard of an elegant apartment complex, also built in the early 1920s, arched stone entryways, a roof of red clay tiles, Kat's building. Over here, there was grass you could go barefoot in. The children played in a wading pool. The mothers drank white wine out of plastic cups. The lowering sun cast a glow over them. Beyond the fence: a car dealership, the four-lane rush of Northern Boulevard, LaGuardia. A plane or two would cut through the sky. But the fence was high, overgrown with vines, and this spot was a secret they were grateful to share.

To think that they'd been strangers so recently. Self-selecting into a group of neighborhood parents (mostly mothers) who all had newborns around the same time. They got so lucky, they said, earnestly. Justine wasn't sure how she would have handled the early weeks and months, the whole first year, without them. How tender she'd been that year, how moved by the smallest of kindnesses: Oliver's pediatrician, an elderly Argentine with the air of an old-world statesman, appearing at the hospital to check on the newborn, turning to her and asking, "And how is the queen?" And when Oliver had cried so inconsolably those first months, the doctor had said "He's a passionate person," and it had seemed like a beneficent prophecy. The time when Justine returned from a long walk in the neighborhood with Oliver in the stroller—the only way he would nap—and a procedural show had started filming in the vestibule of their building. The crew might have made her wait outside and Oliver would have woken up—disaster. But the actress in the scene waved Justine through and offered to help carry the stroller up the lobby stairs. Justine could have cried. She developed an outsize fondness for the actress. She rooted for her in anything she appeared in.

It had been an infancy for all these new mothers, too. These new mothers with their new children. Mothering each other. Sometimes it seemed they were isolated in a distant colony, on the moon, these infant-mothers. Long enough so they became aliens to their own world on earth. They returned, eventually, and re-assimilated. But it wasn't easy, and for some of them, the re-assimilation was ongoing.

Years later, rearranging a room, Justine would find a notebook in which she had kept a log of her newborn's sleep: when and where and for how long each day. Had she read a book that instructed her to do this? She didn't remember. It looked like the work of a not-sane person. Which is maybe what she had been.

By all appearances, Justine had re-assimilated. Gone back to work, established the inviolable routines that structured a day, and by extension, a life. And yet sometimes those routines, if she stopped to examine them, struck her as precarious and arbitrary. The routines made it easy to avoid examination. That was their purpose. If she stuck to them, she didn't have to think about the precarity, the arbitrariness, of her life. The threat that one event—losing her job, a health scare, an accident with Ollie, God forbid—would upend it all. The routines pushed the threat of precarity into the corner. But it was there, waiting. How easily things could fall apart. And when she had heard the news about James—the memorial was now one week ago—the precarity made its presence known once more. The tremor created by his death seemed to expose or create a crack into which she might slip. Into which some irrational part of her wanted to go?

Her move to place herself within James's death, in the story of it or the aftermath—going to the memorial, reaching out to Marina—struck her as a sort of experiment or test, to see how close she could draw herself into the precarity without succumbing to it. Where was the line? If you crossed it, could you cross back? The way she'd jumped, over text, at Marina's invitation to meet up soon, had to do with this: *Can you draw me once again into a flow of youth? Not even my youth—I don't want to go back to that, exactly—but youth itself, the pulsating thing itself?*

JAMES HADN'T CLEARED everything out of their place, Marina's place, before he left. Most of it, but Marina found a box that he'd either forgotten to move into storage or meant to come back for. A random assortment of notebooks, a pair of hiking boots, an old manual Nikon, swim shorts. (The dip in his lower back, on the beach, as he faced the water.) She opened one of the notebooks, with interest and trepidation— what if it were a personal journal?—but it contained years-old field notes, reporting notes. She kept one of them, to have this record of his handwriting, and asked Rafael if he'd like the other things. He said yes.

She'd long thought that Rafael and James shared an attitude, a kind of carelessness with their lives, that they each encouraged in the other, which sometimes played out as a lack of ego, but which could also be seen as selfish. If you are careless with your life, how careful are you with the lives of those you love? James went off and took pictures. Rafael—she wasn't even sure what exactly he did. He was an artist who had moved into furniture design. Or a furniture designer who had moved into art? In any case, he made furniture and had recently undertaken a sort of performance project that involved traveling to budget hotel breakfasts around the country, wearing a "freedom" t-shirt, gauging reactions.

As Rafael had said at the memorial, James found this project a little thin, too knowing. And Marina agreed with James, but maybe she had missed something, in Rafael.

She carried the box of things from the subway, down rickety stairs with their peeling green paint, out of the shadow of the elevated tracks. Buildings of two or three stories lined the streets, brick and vinyl siding. Ridgewood. Rafael lived three flights up in an older, stone building, rundown from the outside and in the linoleum-lined corridors. But when he opened his door all she saw were tall windows and sun on the floor. One of those temperate Saturdays in September that invite you to stay in as much as go out.

How nice it was, his place. He said he'd lived there for years. He'd had time to make it his own. Sparely furnished, light crossing along the far wall.

"Thanks for coming out here," he said.

"Yeah. How is it that I've never been here before?"

"I don't know." With his hands in his pockets, he raised his shoulders, widened his eyes. Had it been James? Had he not wanted to bring her to Rafael's home? "I'm not much of a host, maybe. But here," he said, moving to take the box from her. When their hands touched, she had to admit to herself what had made her keen enough to take the train all the way over here to deliver a box of things that could have just as easily stayed in the back of her closet. And was he aware of it?

He took the box and set it down on a table she assumed he'd designed himself. It looked like his work, what she'd seen of it—wood and powder-coated metal, clean lines. Neither of them took a seat, though, in the matching chairs. Everything in here dispelled that old idea of him as careless. Even the limited-edition sneakers he had on. She'd noticed his sneaker fascination before, though now it struck her as more voluptuary and more meticulous. The way another person might parcel out a piece of chocolate or a glass of red wine. Just so. It was connoisseurship—a world he moved in that had its own subcultural codes she recognized existed even if she didn't completely understand what they were or what they meant.

He kept moving, over to the kitchen, a countertop along a wall. She stood still, her hands in the pockets of her dress.

"Can I get you anything?" he asked.

"Who said you weren't much of a host? I'll have some water. Thanks."

No, not careless at all.

"You were really good up there at the memorial," she said, and immediately regretted it. He hadn't been performing a comedy set. "I mean what you said. It was moving."

"It's a weird talent. Public speaking at funerals. I don't know why but I seem to be good at it." Bringing the water over, handing her a glass.

"Have you been to a lot?"

"Funerals? Not even. A few older relatives, a former professor of mine. But never anyone, like, our age. My age, I should say." He was a few years younger than James, she recalled, and so, a few years older than her. "You didn't want to get up and say anything?"

She shook her head. "I couldn't very well follow you."

Had she ever even talked to Rafael without James around? Had a real conversation of any length? No, despite having spent a good deal of time in Rafael's presence. James had always been there.

"The camera looks valuable," he said, taking it from the box on the table. "Are you sure you don't want it?"

"Would you want to sell it?" she asked.

"No. I'd probably keep it. And I don't mean to automatically reduce everything to its monetary value. Fuck capitalism." He said the last bit with a percussive emphasis of both protest and irony. He spoke like a growing number of people she knew did those days: an outward antipathy toward excess and structural inequality and an acute inner awareness of what things cost and what they were economically worth.

"What about the hiking boots?" she asked. "Donation?"

"Maybe. They should fit me, though. We were the same shoe size."

"I don't know, they don't totally seem like your style."

"What's my style?"

She said she didn't know, but she'd already revealed her hand.

"I don't only wear fashion sneakers, Marina."

"Really?" She looked at the ones he was wearing.

"I've even been out hiking in the woods before. Real woods, with actual, like, trees."

"And trails?"

"Those too."

A smile in his voice, in his eyes, when she met them with her own. She wanted to tell him how it still reverberated with her that he looked her way when he finished talking at the memorial, when nobody else but Holly seemed to understand that she might not have wanted to speak but she nevertheless wanted acknowledgment. It had been a couple of weeks since then. Not long, though already, time had been defined and divided. They were now in the time when routine, or what looked like it, was supposed to start returning, no?

"Does it seem to you like James is still traveling?" she asked. "Like he's just away on assignment?"

This was almost becoming a line, what she thought she should say, to fill conversational space. She expected Rafael to nod in agreement and regret, as other people did.

"No. Not really. It feels to me like he's gone. And now I have to figure out how to live with that."

He kept his eyes on her. All she could do was look away and drink her water as her chest tightened and color rose to her face. When she glanced back, dared herself to, he'd shifted his gaze.

"I was watching this earlier," he said, and took his phone out of his back pocket to show her a video James had sent while traveling. James hadn't sent it to her, but then he wouldn't have—the kind of casual communication they had decided against when ending things.

Marina saw a group of musicians on a tented stage: three women in black headwraps and long, loose skirts and a man in white singing with handclaps, percussion, and an electric guitar. Tuareg music, Rafael said, of the chugging, incantatory song. He handed her the phone and she sat on his couch. He sat next to her, his bare arm touching hers as they listened.

The trance of the music began to work on her, an enlargement, one of those moments that take you outside yourself, revealing the circumscription of your life and allowing you an opportunity to break from it, if only fleetingly. The feeling that James had once described to her, the feeling he first had as a boy at the Kanes' house in the winter. An expansiveness; obvious maybe—how wide the world was, all these people, all these lives—but not so common as to be unaffecting. Or not so common to her. It was one she appreciated in small doses; James preferred a steady drip. And with that thought, the enlargement shrank and sadness shaded into it. That James had shared this footage with Rafael and not with her.

Rafael must have been aware that she hadn't received this—why else would he have shown it to her—but there seemed to be no smugness on his part, no motivation to make her feel excluded. Realizing he had done just that, he said he was sorry, an apology that could be as broad as it needed to be. She was broadly sorry, too.

They were either going to stay there on the couch, it seemed to her, or she was going to leave. If she looked at him, they would stay on the couch. She didn't look at him. She also didn't get up to go. She raised her water to take another sip but her glass was empty. He'd downed his, too.

Finally, he asked what she had going on for the day. Whether it was curiosity and a way of keeping her there or a hint for her to get moving and leave him to his Saturday, his life, she couldn't be sure.

"Not too much. Errands. Things I have to catch up on. You?"

"I'll probably head to the studio." He gestured toward the table, the work he did.

"Yeah. That's good."

It occurred to her they had no reason to see each other after this, not with any regularity, any intent. She wanted to come up with a reason but nothing plausible flashed in her mind.

To the door, then. And off to the rest of her day.

He thanked her, she thanked him, and they hugged, and he didn't pull away, and when he continued not to pull away, she pressed the side of her face to where his chest curved to his shoulder. His soft t-shirt, his body, strong and exceedingly present, against hers. She moved her hands up under his t-shirt, pressing them to his back, as if to hide or warm them. He had one hand still on her back and with the other lifted her dress and then he was touching her through her underwear.

They didn't go to his bed, the couch was closer. She hadn't anticipated—hadn't known to anticipate—how easily Rafael's body worked with hers. How she would laugh, and he would laugh, too, after, when she was still on top of him and he was still inside her. Another release. The strangeness of that—how they'd fit and how they'd laughed—she'd think, after, retreating alone to his bathroom.

Despite his attractiveness, she'd never imagined sex with Rafael, at least not before the memorial service. Not before James died. She wasn't going to allow herself to believe that James's death had caused this shift, in her, in Rafael, or to allow for the conclusion that they could never have had sex like that if James were still alive. But part of the last clause cut through her consciousness: *sex like that*. Sex like what? Like it would happen again. It had the unfixed quality that sex with James had once had, early on. The thrill of simply feeling a different body on hers, but that wasn't entirely it. With James, in time, she had often gone inside herself to an extent. She didn't feel great about admitting it, but he'd become a body onto whom she could—closing her eyes—project whomever or whatever she liked. With Rafael . . . she had liked looking at him—she couldn't stop looking at him. It had been like that with James, too, at the beginning—that *abandon ship* morning, when she'd wanted to fix him in her mind.

The longer she stayed in the bathroom, on the toilet, the more time she had to turn inward and away from the atmosphere outside of the bathroom, an atmosphere of permission, a suspension of judgment. It was already slipping away and she didn't want it to go. She came out, naked, to find him half-dressed.

She didn't gather her clothes and take them to the bathroom, as she might have. She put them back on, unembarrassed, in the open room. To let him watch her. To make him watch her. And he did.

"So, you're going to your studio?" she said.

"And you have those very important errands."

"They're critical."

She was relieved by his smile, which remained part of the permissive atmosphere.

"I'm glad you came by," he said.

"Me too."

She started to laugh again, though not like before, when she'd been on top of him, when she could feel him laughing, too, when they were laughing into each other.

"Is it really that funny?" he asked.

"No," she answered, still laughing a little. "It's not funny at all."

She made her way to the door. If she gave him a minute, he'd walk out with her. So, she did, and together they went down the dark, quiet stairwell and into the brightness of the day.

THE PICTURE THAT ALEX had taken of Holly, the print of it she'd had framed, now sat in her hall closet, taped up in cardboard from the last time she'd moved. There hadn't been a place for it. Rather, she hadn't felt motivated to find a place for it and so it had stayed leaning against a wall in the dark.

Sitting on the floor of the hallway, she took care to unwrap it, though she wasn't sure what compelled her. The picture itself, the framed object, had become something of a companion. The photographer, Alex, had dropped away, and so it didn't matter what his intention was in taking the picture, how he'd once felt about her, or even how he felt about her now. His embarrassment at the restaurant, his embarrassment at his embarrassment, his anger at that double embarrassment. None of it contaminated the photograph-object.

When she looked at the young woman in it, she still recognized herself. More readily than when she looked in the mirror these days. It wasn't that she wanted to be that young woman again, but that in some sense she still was. What had changed, though, or dissipated, was the angst—no better word for it—of her youth. How badly that young woman, the dancer in that picture, had wanted to be known. She hadn't wanted fame—how many dancers were famous anymore?—but recognition, of her talent, her will. Her existence, really. How it had racked her, how angry it had made her, that lack of recognition. Some fire she was stoking. And the fire never entirely extinguished itself, a small flame had continued to glow, only not so brightly, not with any threat of destruction or violence. It took time and humiliation to put it out: Leaving New York to go back to Boston, her life packed into a borrowed hatchback. The untrained mother of one of her dance students telling her that they would be moving on, that her daughter was ready for "proper" lessons now "from a real professional." A wobbling that developed in her ankle and turned into a sprain. Eventually her drive for recognition began to seem like something that belonged to the photograph, put away for so long.

She still couldn't find a spot on the wall where it would work, where she'd want to put it up and see it every day, so she left it unwrapped but slid it back into the closet, behind the hem of a long winter coat.

Alex had dropped away from the image itself but not from everything surrounding it, the circumstances in which it was taken, or the circumstances Holly found herself in now. For a moment, she wondered what her life would be like if Alex had died instead of James. She didn't wonder—she wished, wished fleetingly, that Alex had died instead of James.

To lose Alex would be to lose the person around whom your idea of yourself takes form. For so long, she had served a dual purpose for Alex, depending on what he needed and when he needed it. She was either the lesser one, the one who couldn't hack it—too sensitive to pressure and to competition—or the better one who didn't need to hack it because she saw through it all, was above it all, outside of it all. It: New York, art, creative success, movement within certain spheres of influence, a system that had worked for him so well he no longer saw it as a system.

He hadn't invented his idea of her wholesale. To a degree, she was both those women, the lesser and the better. And Alex had been, for her, a link to a more glamorous, more ambitious world she never had to fully let go of. She was on the wall of a museum. He was also a reminder of who succeeded in this world and who didn't. Her name was on the little white card next to the portrait but that was all. Alex got a whole bio. When he died, long obituaries would be printed. And histories, certain histories at least, would remember him.

They had all been so young once, part of a scene, or a loose network of scenes, that began to gain attention outside itself and in the process developed its own mythology. Some of them, like Alex, gained public reputations and esteem, if not celebrity. Enough interest, enough support to make art for an audience. Some of them became adjacent to that interest and support, and the rest of them, as they grew up and grew older, became adjacent to the adjacency. She was thinking of the women who had booked acts at dank clubs whose dankness would later be written about in legendary terms, who had played bass in No Wave bands, who painted, who shot video, who took photographs, who danced. They had moved out of the city when they could no longer afford it, had become registered nurses, schoolteachers, halfhearted real estate agents, social workers. Some had had children, others never did. She had never thought of those women as a different kind of loose network, though that's what they were. The women whose work was not in a museum or preserved on a record or printed in a book and never would be because their early efforts had been lost to obscurity or had been ephemeral to begin with. The women who would become footnotes in the more celebrated lives of others.

What was that and why was that? she wondered, trying to untangle a knot of sexism, talent, drive, and . . . was there a word for being at the right place at the right time? And then being at the right place at the right time again and again? Having a knack for that? And was it really a knack? Or was knack effectively shorthand for whole systems of value and identification that created opportunity for some and not for others?

James had had photographs of his on the walls of museums, galleries. Nothing permanent, but there'd been exhibitions. James could hack it. He could withstand pressure. He even required it, at times, for motivation. He was like his mother in that respect, only in Lila that drive never expressed itself in a way that others publicly esteemed, that they gave out assignments or grants and awards for. Nobody ever lauded it in Lila. Holly may have been one of the few people in the world who even recognized it as such.

When Holly had left New York and moved back to Boston—she never seemed to be in the right place at the right time—Lila had been happy and welcoming, excited, even. You're home! But behind that, so subtly that only her sister might perceive it, was a sense of disappointment, for Holly and for herself. Holly, who had lit out with such high expectations, had returned with those expectations unmet. It diminished her in Lila's eyes. *You were supposed to do great things for us, Holly, because I didn't or couldn't and now I have James.* There was a whiff of failure, of defeat, around Holly. It hurt Lila's pride.

Holly had wanted to say, at the time: It's not my fault you are where you are, Lila. You can be disappointed *for* me, but you have no right to be disappointed *by* me. And great things, Lila? You have the great thing: you have James.

Lila would have accepted the logic of that of course, if not the emotional truth. But Holly said nothing to this effect. Lila's pride—where and how did she derive it?—had always entranced Holly, from the time they were girls. She didn't want to question or undercut her older sister, because Holly knew she would need to rely on that pride now, learn to draw from it like a well, if she were to build a life back here.

Combined with Lila's pride, which had rooted for Holly, was her first-rate bullshit detection, which Holly had always felt she was up against. First-rate in that contemptuous and affectionate way that develops when you spend so much time growing up in the company of bullshitters. Men who repeatedly had a hand, to a degree, in larcenous schemes, and women who looked the other way, except when they looked at each other. One or two Lady Macbeths, even. Most of them, including Holly's parents, would die before they turned 65, of heart attacks or cancer. They never got too elderly, and Holly thought of the women always in trench coats and handkerchiefs tied over their heads at the napes of their necks. The men in slacks, hair slicked. All of them with that unerring ability (save for a few key blind spots) to pinpoint fraudulence, sanctimony, and pretension. Lila had acquired it by osmosis, it seemed. But with that came a certain rigidity, an intolerance of sorts. What Holly had loved about going away and going to New York was the release from that rigidity. To be around other people who would understand, if not celebrate, her pretensions, who wouldn't laugh her out of the room. In Holly's mind, to the extent that Lila's bullshit detection outweighed the pride, and to the extent that her parents, who had been too proud to laugh at her most prized pretensions, were no longer around, Lila had come to stand for all of Boston. And to be "home," Holly had feared, was to exist under a frustrating, limiting scrutiny.

She would discover, though, that James had loosened something in Lila. It was as if helplessness, which had frightened her, disgusted her even, now increasingly touched Lila. As Holly always saw it, Lila could deal with or handle whatever came her way, and her sympathy for people who struggled to deal didn't extend too far. But how helpless James was! How vulnerable and innocent. Instead of seeing herself and her capacity to endure whatever shit might be thrown at her, it was as if she began to ask why James—why anyone—should have to endure having shit thrown at them in the first place.

For two months, Holly lived in Lila's apartment, on a couch, before she moved into her own place only a couple of blocks away. She got to know her then four-year-old nephew and got to know her sister anew, taking on as much of the childcare as she could. Preschool drop-offs and pickups, trips to the park, game-playing, cooking, cleaning, bathing, putting to bed. Dancing with James, too. If she was burdened at times, more often she conceived of their lives together as a matriarchal society of three. Lila's living room became a remote island which they ruled. It struck her as improvisational and experimental and ancient all at once.

As James grew older, her involvement lessened, and when Lila moved James to a suburb with better schools, it became even more attenuated. But Lila and James had given Holly a purpose she'd never had. Before them, her own ambition and initiative had served as purpose enough for her. Which is why the whiff of failure hurt so much, depriving her of her own sense of self. And then, just when a state of passivity lay ready to enfold her, there were Lila and James, requesting her attention and offering their own in return.

Holly had closed the closet door on the photograph, moved from the hallway to her kitchen table, wooden and scratched, well-loved, where James had sat with her now and then, where Lila had sat with her, too.

She had to remind herself she had friends, people in her life, the occasional lover. She had the loose network. She had some other family, too, but distant, in ways both geographic and genealogic. For years—until Lila got sick, really—neither Lila nor James had been the center of her focus. They hadn't been her whole life. How could they be her whole life in death?

IN HER JUNIOR YEAR OF ART SCHOOL, Justine took a leave of absence for one semester, followed by one more. She went home to live with her parents and worked for a cleaning service. She was relating this to Marina in order to get to a relevant point, but to get to the point required a digression on this late September afternoon, under a bright blue sky, in the fading green of Central Park.

"Did you ever snoop?" Marina asked.

"Around houses I cleaned?" If Justine considered it a bit of an odd or loaded question, she attributed it to a lack of formality on Marina's part, that forwardness she'd shown at the memorial service. "Sure. Yeah. But not even in an active way. It was all just there, these private things you just observe."

Justine had been interested, obviously, in what she saw. But so much of it came and went and didn't stay with her. With one exception.

"There was this girl," she said.

She told Marina how they would arrive, four of them, as a team. They'd park the bright green minivan in suburban driveways. They had a set schedule and regular clients. But the nature of the setup encouraged anonymity; clients communicated largely with their team's boss and were out of the house when they showed up during the day. They never met the people who lived in the places they cleaned, though they saw their pictures, knew which shampoo and condoms they used, which medications they took. And despite, or maybe because, the four of them were routinely immersed in the intimate, domestic worlds of others, they all got along well enough but never really bonded outside of the job. Nobody wanted to make more of it than it was. They shook their heads at the wasteful or the ridiculous but then they put away what they'd witnessed, like bills in a wallet, and got on with things.

Every other week they would go to a house at the end of a winding, wooded drive in a long-established, affluent neighborhood that afforded its inhabitants a balance between seclusion and accessibility. You couldn't hear the train, which took commuters straight into the city, but the station wasn't too far to walk to.

This home had been built by a mid-century modernist: boxy and U-shaped, an exterior of dark wood siding, and spans of tall plate glass that revealed—when the floor-to-ceiling curtains were open—expensively but comfortably furnished rooms. The owners had paintings on the walls and art books on side tables. Good art books, Justine noted. At the center of the bottom of the U was the showstopper, glass walls built around a living tree whose branches reached up beyond the roof.

A family lived in this house. The father moved out over the course of the time Justine worked there. His belongings disappeared from the top of the bureau, the desk in the office. The mother, it seemed, took to rearranging in his absence, moving furniture, lamps. They had one daughter, and though the cleaning team never met the husband or the wife when they worked on the house, the girl was often there, in her room at one tip of the U-shape. Her mother's bedroom, a quiet temple of thick white carpet, occupied the other end.

The girl would arrive home from high school, in baggy sweaters and jeans, alone, and head straight to her room, saying hello to them softly through a veil of embarrassment, and, in the hunched way she carried herself, some hatred of being put in this position. It galled this girl that her parents, her mother, lived in this large house that needed cleaning and that they had better things to do than to be here while it was being cleaned. It galled this girl to be the one left to face up to her family's mortifying privilege. It galled her that she had the personality that she did. Another girl might have been out doing something illicit and wild, an afternoon hour or two that would never have to be accounted for.

"You don't have to do my room, if that's okay," she said, opening her door when Justine knocked, only enough to make brief eye contact.

"If you're sure," Justine said, wanting to offer something other than a polite, understanding half-smile and nod, though nothing else seemed appropriate. Justine went to work on the bathroom, the girl's bathroom, which never revealed much. Anything too expressive she must have kept in her room.

Once, in late fall when dead leaves had been swept into piles on the lawn, as they were getting back into their van Justine saw through a wide, uncovered window that the girl had come out of her room. She wore a black sweatshirt, carried a bag of chips toward a giant TV, which Justine had just dusted, and laid herself down on the couch. It was as if she were unfurling, finally, now that she could, now that they were gone. She reminded Justine, at first, of a bear nosing around a vacated campsite. Blundering but forceful, dominating in the absence of humans. But as she watched her sink into the couch, the girl reminded Justine more of the tree growing through the glass.

"I quit that job when I went back to school and I never saw the girl again after that, but I've wondered what ever happened to her," Justine told Marina. "In a way, I think of James the way I thought of this girl, if that makes sense. This girl whose name I never even knew. But I felt for her. She had this lasting effect on me. I kept seeing myself in relation to her."

"There are people in your life, every so often, that you share an intimacy with and then never see again," said Marina. They were making their way around the eastern edge of the Reservoir, and into a northern part of the park Marina rarely visited now but had known well. Central Park itself no longer figured in her everyday orientation. Her parents had sold the classic six and moved an hour north to a house along the Hudson. This uptown area: for therapists, museums, private schools, and a place, maybe, to meet people like Justine.

"So, you know what I mean," said Justine.

"I think so," said Marina.

"James never mentioned me," said Justine.

"No," said Marina. "But that doesn't mean much. I'm not sure how it would've come up."

"Yeah. I never mentioned James to my husband. Until I heard about his death."

"Maybe James would have brought you up, at some point. It wasn't like he deliberately kept things from me or kept things to himself. That was never our problem."

"What was it then? Your problem."

"Probably what you would expect. I guess I was a different person at the beginning of our relationship than I was toward the end." She spoke of wanting a little more predictability, a sense of knowing what to expect. More than he could give her, which upset him because he gave her all he could. And then maybe he needed what she couldn't give him, an understanding she could never share of what he'd witnessed in his work. "I mean, I would never want that experience, if I had a choice. And is that willful ignorance on my part? Or just self-preservation and fucking common sense?"

Marina spoke calmly, as if voicing thoughts she had been over in her mind but hadn't said aloud.

"I don't know," said Justine. Like Marina, she had no strong desire to see what James saw. And she wasn't sure what that made her. A bad person? An inattentive one? A coward? A realist?

"How did you and James meet?" Justine asked.

"At a party." Better to say, for the integrity of parties everywhere, a university function? In a hall with high ceilings and windows that looked out onto a courtyard of mature trees and concrete slabs to sit on. Crowded for this type of thing. Hot, even. One of the last warm days of the year. He had his shirt sleeves rolled. She didn't remember who introduced them, but there they were, drinks in hand, eyes on each other. And they talked, only to each other, long enough to finish their drinks and he asked if he could get her another and then, if you could believe it, returned with one.

Communications officer? he'd said. Like a cop? Of communications?

Officer as in one who works in an office.

As quickly as she could, to get it out of the way, she explained what she did at work and he didn't seem bored. He was also not bored when he spoke about his own role at the university, his students. It was relatively new for him, being an educator, at least in any official capacity. And it was a different life—a different rhythm and pace—than what he'd been used to. But he liked it, appreciated how it could accommodate his photographic work, the larger, longer projects not so strictly tied to the news cycles that had him chasing stories all over the place, at any time.

Academia as a refuge from diminished opportunities in the media landscape, she thought. A phrase she'd heard or read somewhere. Academia was less a refuge now and more of a diminished opportunity itself, but it roughly applied.

"Academia as a refuge from diminished opportunities in the media landscape," she said.

"I never thought I wanted or needed a refuge, but as refuges go . . ."

When people pressed into their conversation, when they had to pretend to draw their attention elsewhere, it was as if only the two of them understood that it was a performance and that when this public scene concluded, they would continue offstage.

And almost as if it were part of the performance, or as if to test the performance, she went out to the courtyard, mingled a bit as the sun went down, sat on one of the slab benches. She placed her glass of white wine on the concrete form, where the condensation on the bottom left a dark ring. Her hands in her lap, arching her back to look over her shoulder, looking around to see if he was still there. Happy to find that he was.

They exchanged numbers and she went home alone but not entirely alone—a giddiness accompanied her.

She looked him up, found his work. He wasn't, in his own words, in an interview she read, particularly skilled at capturing landscape or place—with the exception, perhaps, of people within a vastness, made minuscule by their surroundings, or people rendered in the close-up of chaos. He belonged to an international agency that provided images to news and nongovernmental organizations. He had been so many places: Tunisia during the Arab Spring, the Gulf Coast after Hurricane Katrina, the Crimean region of Ukraine. She looked at his photographs: The family of a Russian political prisoner. A middle-aged woman walking a dog in a bombed-out street somewhere in the Middle East. Bored Kurdish kids sitting with their parents in an institutional setting, a courtroom or small assembly hall lit by a harsh but dull fluorescence.

If he was looking her up online, he'd likely find a few short stories she'd written that she didn't hate enough to request they be removed from the sites that had published them. She had a feeling he would like them because he already liked her, though possibly they'd make him like her less.

She thought his work was captivating. But she really thought, *Oh I can't do this. Not with this guy.* He must possess some seriousness of purpose she didn't have (that maybe came with age? Oh God, was he going to try to "educate" or "mentor" her?). If there was a spectrum with dogmatic, ideological energy on one end and laziness on the other, they must occupy fairly distant points. *I like sleep and TV and hot water too much to pretend otherwise,* she thought. *He'll catch me out.*

There was a whole conversation about the type of work James did. It touched on imagery and authenticity and voyeurism and objectification and exploitation and meaning itself. It went high, it went low. But did it illuminate him at all for her? Because that was what she was interested in: him. She read a book of interviews with photographers who shot images of war in Iraq, in Afghanistan; so much was the color of clay. The occasional green of palm trees or light blue of a burqa. Out of a dozen interviewed photographers, a handful were women, and it was their words that made the most sense to Marina.

"One of them talked about painting her nails, washing her hair on a day off, to get the dust and dirt out of it, and that felt more real to me than any of the analysis the male photographers applied to their work," she said to Justine. "I understood the experience of the women, I trusted it. The men kind of remained a mystery to me, the way they spoke of the camera being a *device of detachment.*" Marina made quotes with her fingers.

"So, I met James for a movie about a week later. And I wasn't sure if I should tell him about these interviews I'd read. You know, I didn't want to come off as over-invested. But I wanted to know if he was like those male photographers. If he was going to be unknowable in that way. Anyway, I was early and the movie theater was near the shop that sold this fancy deodorant I liked, so I went over there and as I was waiting to buy it, I heard someone call my name from farther back in the line. It was him. He had some face lotion. And then it was like that was all it took, a shared love of overpriced personal care products."

"It's funny," said Justine, "I remember not wanting to come off as too materialistic or consumeristic in front of James. Like he'd be a little disapproving and monastic. But he was never monastic. He had that motorcycle."

"He didn't have a motorcycle when I knew him. But I know what you're saying. That you worried he might be *too* high-minded for you. There was some complication there."

"I think, at the time when I knew him, I tended to see things in starker terms," said Justine. "And it took me a while to understand complications and contradictions. I remember a conversation with him, I was talking about that moment, after college, in New York, when you realize who is secretly wealthy. You don't see it through any obvious ostentation but through who has to hustle and who doesn't. In school, you knew who did work-study, who had loans, and that sort of thing, and maybe you knew whose families were especially well off, but you didn't really know how wealth translated outside that cloistered world. And James was like, *You didn't?* Because he already did, had known for a while, forever, and was wondering what took me so long to see it."

Marina, whom Justine would probably classify at "secretly wealthy," smiled to herself. She'd always had the same reaction to such awakenings as James, though from the opposite side. An almost in-built consciousness about class, and how it delineated time and determined perspective. She and James had understood each other on that level. The solidly middle-class outlook, Justine's outlook, in which that burgeoning consciousness came as a revelation and an outrage, was more alien to her, as it had been to James.

"Anyway," said Justine.

"Anyway," Marina echoed.

The sky was larger up here, this far north in the park. The dimensions of the paths, the trees, the grass, the stones, the ironwork, the streetlamps, seemed slightly different to Marina, as if she were in a foreign country. The same materials, same elements, but put together in a way no longer thoroughly familiar to her eye. Snack wrappers and soda can litter had yet to be swept up. The tourists up here weren't American.

"Can I ask you something?" Marina turned to Justine, who nodded, eyebrows up. "Why did you take those semesters off in college? If you don't mind."

"Oh, no, it's fine." Justine pointed to a bench where they sat, crossing legs, getting comfortable. Justine took a breath, twisted up her hair and then let it fall again. "I got anxious. Like, severe anxiety. Not sleeping. Barely eating. Sweating and shitting weird. Suicidal thoughts because I just wanted that fear to end." She looked toward her feet, toward people passing on the path, not at Marina. "I had to go home and get treatment for it. And then once I was managing it, but still at home, I started cleaning houses. It was meditative, in a way. Maybe also because I knew, or I hoped, that it was temporary for me—the house cleaning—it was like a form of convalescence."

It wasn't a secret. Justine had talked about that time, the extreme edges of it, with other people. But had she ever brought it up so smoothly? Even the weird shitting? In the past, with Adam, discussing that period of her life had been a tender thing; she hadn't known quite how he would react and she had cared so deeply about the outcome. But here, with Marina, she became both matter-of-fact and divulging, assuming a level of intimacy whose origins she could only trace to having known James and to having lost him.

"Did it ever come back?" Marina asked. "The anxiety?"

"Not quite that bad. But I had some trouble post-partum."

She thought better of volunteering those details, not because she was uncomfortable sharing them with Marina, but out of some sense that Marina might be numb to it. That it was a language Justine was fluent in now, speaking it with other mothers, but she understood it was a foreign language that Marina might choose never to learn. And Marina didn't ask her to elaborate.

They stood back up and moved fluidly, in tandem, around Nordic families with their phones out for pictures. Their movement, unhurried but steady, matching their flow of talk. No particular destination but a continual progression. It had been a long time, but Justine recognized this pattern—from the years when she was a lonely person and she would meet someone she wanted to keep talking to. Once, at the end of December, she walked for blocks with the son of a famous writer Marina had probably read—all the way from the Guggenheim down to Houston—talking, talking, as the day turned to night and he left to go meet his celebrated mother for dinner. New Year's Eve was in two days. They spent it together that year, but only that year, and she never met his celebrated mother.

"Do you remember Rafael?" Marina asked. "From the memorial? James's friend. He got up and spoke last."

"I think I do. Yeah."

Marina described how Rafael, over the course of the last two years, had taken to traveling across the country—for work sometimes, or to see people he knew—always by car. He would stay in budget hotels just off the highway, places with uniform, anonymous rooms and where a complimentary buffet breakfast could be had: plastic dispensers of cereal, a chafing dish lined with one massive scrambled egg, another one with processed meat. On occasion, a waffle-making station. Sweet, watery juice and thin coffee. Within sight of any table were one or two TV screens attached high on the wall, broadcasting local news or the weather. The people who availed themselves of the meal were families, mostly, and often a Christian missionary group in matching t-shirts printed with the name of their organization on the front, a verse of scripture on the back. And just as there was always juice and coffee, there was always an older, heavyset white woman with short, graying hair and a face Rafael could only describe as hard yet jowly, mean. He assumed, with some condescension, that all these women had had difficult lives and had reached a stage of what they probably understood to be earned spite. What he thought was interesting though, again with some condescension, was that these women typically wore t-shirts that were ill-fitting but in colors that seemed deliberately chosen: turquoise or bright pink, maybe there was a flower design or appliqué on it. As if the colors were meant to flatter their eyes or complexion. Some consideration, he concluded, and maybe even a pinch of something approaching pleasure, had gone into their appearance, a look which otherwise struck him as utilitarian and practical and devoid, whether out of choice or necessity, of joy.

If it wasn't his first morning at the first hotel with the complimentary breakfast, it was soon after it that he saw a man wearing a t-shirt, gray with a rippling American flag and the word FREEDOM on it. The man, whose long cargo shorts accentuated his beefiness and whose camo baseball cap sat tight on his head, appeared to be related to one of the mean-faced women. Her son or nephew. There was an aggressiveness, a combativeness to the t-shirt. It was a dare, and at the same time, in an authoritarian, threatening way, a warning, intended to keep everyone in their place, or what he believed was their place.

"Freedom," said Justine.

"Freedom," Marina echoed.

James's friend had sat there drinking his coffee, looking over every now and then at the man in the t-shirt, who'd commandeered a table for his family. He thought about the sweatshop where the t-shirt was most likely made, he thought about how this man's freedom and the "freedom" the man was telegraphing, came at the expense of so many other people, if not his own (Rafael's father was Mexican, his mother's family were New Yorkers by way of Puerto Rico). He didn't say anything to the man, angered by own his silence, his in- action, the powerlessness that the man had wanted him to feel. But then the next day, at the next hotel, he saw another white man of similar build at breakfast in another t-shirt with a bald eagle and a gun on it, seated at a table with another pear-shaped, mean-faced older woman. His anger didn't dis- sipate so much as twist itself into a dark laugh.

The next time he was online, he found the same gray t-shirt with the rippling American flag and the word "free- dom" and ordered a few. He was putting together a costume, of sorts, for when he would travel to these spots outside cit- ies. He would wear the shirt to each breakfast he attended. He'd have on the unbranded, limited-edition sneakers he favored, which he figured might be mistaken for orthopedic walking shoes.

Justine laughed. There's more, said Marina's expression.

What they noticed, the people at the breakfasts, was that he wasn't the type who'd normally wear that shirt. He didn't look the part at all.

"So, he's taking back freedom?" said Justine. "Taking back the freedom shirt?"

"It's a kind of performance art," said Marina. Only he doesn't take pictures or make videos of it or anything. He documents it after the fact, with a photo of himself and, like, a journal entry. He's fucking with people, with their assump- tions. I guess."

"And he hasn't gotten shot?"

"Not yet. But he got written up in some art thing. Something like he was interrogating the hallucinatory trope of the American road in a tumultuous era of xenophobia, ra- cial injustice, surveillance, and climate change."

Justine considered this. She recalled Rafael at the memorial service, how he'd been talking about a project that James had judged a little slick, a little obvious—it must have been this.

How much, she wondered, had James's outlook influenced Marina's opinions?

"What about the other people who are there just eating breakfast on the way to somewhere else and not wearing politically charged t-shirts?" Justine asked. "Does he feel any responsibility toward those people?"

"I don't know. I think if there's an argument he's trying to make, it's an anarchic one. He's trying to get at the absurdity of it all, which is also the danger of it all? It's not really an argument, it's not polemical, it's more of an aesthetic investigation. To question the meaning of the word, freedom, and the meaning of wearing a shirt with that word on it, and the meaning of having to look at such a shirt while you're eating a mediocre buffet breakfast in a place that could be anywhere in the middle of nowhere. And eventually, he has to include and implicate himself in that loop of meaning. You know, at what point does he just become an asshole?"

"Is that rhetorical or are you really asking?"

"Both, I think," said Marina. They'd passed the manicured Conservatory Gardens and made their way toward the Harlem Meer, where men, mostly, no longer tourists, stood along the water's edge with fishing rods and tackle. Marina and Justine headed for the top of a large rock overlooking the glinting lake and sat, alone, up high. The grass was green, still, and overgrown.

"I don't want him to be an asshole," said Marina. "I had sex with him."

"Oh," said Justine, with the objectivity of a journalist—interested, taking notes, but revealing no judgment. Justine wasn't sure she had a judgment to reveal. Only that she remembered what that was like, in a different phase of her life: sex with new people that wasn't necessarily uncomplicated but happened easily and often enough.

"Not when I was with James," Marina quickly added. "But after. Like a week ago. I don't know, is that worse?"

Justine stared off at a distant tree, as if it would supply an answer.

"Well, what is it that you feel bad about or ashamed of?"

"Nothing, really. And I think I'm ashamed that I'm not ashamed. And does that make me liberated and easygoing or does it make me a sociopath?"

Justine laughed; Marina didn't.

"I wouldn't say easygoing, no. Or you wouldn't even be asking the question. Are you gonna see him again?"

"I don't want to have to go to bad hotel breakfasts with the guy in the performative freedom t-shirt. But I'd like to have sex with him again."

"Asked and answered, then."

"And even that's not true. I'm making him into 'the guy in the performative t-shirt.' I don't want to do that. He was the only one—the only person—at James's memorial who even thought to mention me." Marina paused. "And you know, at least he's doing it, he's putting something out there. And I can sit here and mock it but that feels pretty shitty pretty quickly. Because what the fuck have I ever done? What the fuck do I do?"

"You write, don't you?"

"Yeah, but who doesn't?"

"I don't."

"Well, actually, I don't either. Or I mean, I haven't lately. And 'lately' is starting to stretch it."

Justine, who basically only doodled now, understood. The last works of any worth that she'd done had been drawings that she framed for Ollie's room. They elicited a bittersweet pang whenever she might pause and look at them, some mixture of admiration and promise and failure and love.

On the rock, Justine leaned back on her palms, and then lay her body all the way down. Marina followed. All they saw was sky.

"Holly, James's aunt, offered to read something of mine, if I wanted," said Marina. "And at first I felt terrible that I didn't have anything I wanted to show her. But then I felt motivated. To produce something."

Justine closed her eyes, flung her arm over her face. Still listening.

"Holly wants me to go with her when she scatters his ashes," said Marina. "She asked me and I didn't know how to answer her. I haven't said one way or the other yet. I'm not sure he'd want me there, want me to be part of that, given things between us."

"But Holly wants you to be part of it."

"Would she want me there if she knew about Rafael?"

"I would bet yes. I would bet it makes no difference to her wanting you there."

Even as the sun sank westward, the day would remain warm into the evening. It was early fall, but summer's heat was hanging on and they were two women on a rock in the middle of a city. Maybe it was the turn their conversation had taken; ever so briefly, the who and the where and the when of herself slipped away for Justine. The precarity, whose hum had grown louder since she heard about James, was silenced.

Her moorings came back quickly enough, and not without a measure of guilt.

"Adam has had Oliver most of the day." Justine sat up. "I should be getting back."

Off the rock, along a path, out of the park. They took the Fifth Avenue bus downtown. Next to each other in two seats, Marina at the window, Justine by the aisle.

"What was your first impression of me?" Marina asked. "At the memorial."

"Interesting lawyer," Justine said.

Marina's full and unguarded laugh. Justine's loud smile.

"Though that wasn't at the memorial. I have to admit, I saw pictures of you online beforehand."

"Of course."

"What was your first impression of me?"

"I don't know, exactly. You looked about as lonely as I felt, standing by that painting. But mostly you just seemed . . . nice? You seemed nice."

IN BED, JUSTINE ROLLED INTO ADAM, into the fleshy softness of his arm and the muscular strength of it. If this were to disappear? No getting beyond that question. Dread like a building or a boulder she couldn't see past. She simply had to move on from the thought.

Sunday morning. Early but the sun was already up, coming in off the street and through the bedroom curtains.

"People," she murmured.

"People," he said.

Any minute, Oliver would totter in and Justine would say, "Where did you come from?" and he'd say, "I came from my bed."

And there he was, his peachy skin glowing, his mop of curls matted with sleep. He climbed up between the two of them. Oliver's face against hers. If she could hold to the disappearing moment—but there was breakfast to make and Oliver was already rolling over her and lowering himself off the bed.

"I still have to tell you about yesterday, about Marina," Justine said to Adam in the strip of space that was their kitchen.

"Tell me."

"I really liked her. She had this very easy way about her. Easy to be around." She told him how they were two women on a rock in the middle of the city.

"You know what she's not like? She's not fake mellow."

"Fake mellow is the worst." He got the coffee going. "When someone thinks they're easygoing, but you can feel the anxiety coming off of them."

"Yes. Give me a tightly wound anxious person who knows it over a fake mellow one any day." She poured cereal into bowls. "I don't even understand fake mellow. People like that always trip me up because at first you go with it and then, once you're feeling comfortable—*mellow*, even—you say something that sets them on edge because they're really pretty rigid in their outlook."

"They don't really see beyond themselves. As soon as something doesn't fit with their mentality, they make you feel wrong."

She lifted Oliver into his booster seat at the table. Adam stood by the counter. *This is happening, this is where I am*, she thought, that echo that recurred throughout her life. That had crossed her mind the night she'd slept with James. Then: *This is my room with the rotting floor and his hands are on me and we are going to have sex.* Now: *That is my husband, and this is my child, we are a family and we live here.*

The instant passed. They ate, cleaned up, dressed for a day where they didn't have much to do, though there was always something you had to do with a three-year-old. They headed over to the farmers' market a few blocks away by the park, out of some desire not for the thing itself but for the desire to want it, to be the people who stocked their kitchen well and supported local agriculture. Whatever pleasure they might derive from the experience was so often undercut by the self-congratulatory mood of the whole enterprise, the theatricality of it, the performance they were required to participate in.

She walked past people and overheard:

"I made such a good aioli with this garlic last week!"

"Are you sure you grabbed enough asparagus, babe?"

"Oh, no, it couldn't be easier. You just brush it with butter, a little salt, and then roast it. Theo can't get enough."

Justine watched Theo, she assumed, peer over a table and press his fingers into a zucchini bread as if he were giving it a deep tissue massage, while his father continued enthusing to a friend.

Compelled to mimic the excitement, she would then feel deficient for not genuinely being excited and then spiteful for being made to feel that deficiency. It made her want to stand on the corner, disdainfully smoking a cigarette, though she'd never smoked. It made her think of Eileen/Irene. The fish, the greens, the local honey and eggs were meant to make up for that deficiency, soothe the spite. Sometimes they did. There was a doughnut vendor, if all else failed. They could pass an hour, maybe two, and Oliver could run around in the park and nap well in the afternoon.

Outside on the corner they saw Kat and Kat's daughter Lu and a plan was made. Adam would run home and put their perishables in the fridge, Kat's too, and then come back and meet them. Justine knew he'd take more time than was strictly necessary, lingering at home. She would have done so. And anyway, Adam was owed this break, because he'd been on duty most of the previous day, when Justine was out being a woman high up on a rock in the middle of the city. Momentarily forgetting herself.

Justine and Kat had spent so much time together with their children. Months of contradiction, in which an overarching tentativeness, a feeling for one's way, came up against seemingly endless, unchanging stretches of hours. In Kat's car they drove out to Flushing, to the Hall of Science and along the BQE to Eastern Parkway to go to the Brooklyn Museum one ambitious morning, because it would be "good to see some art." (The wailing infants disagreed.) Very early on, they spent a rainy day at a Great Neck mall, pushing their strollers along marble floors hoping their children would sleep. (The obsession with sleep!) All that time they must have talked—the bond of motherhood so instantly opened lines of communication. But there was always a subtle barrier Justine couldn't breach. Maybe it was a question of disposition. Disposition toward revelation, which required trust in order to be brought out. She trusted Kat but suspected that Kat, on some level, must not fully trust her. Yes, they wholly entrusted their children to each other, but not their innermost concerns. In comparison, how quickly, how intimately she and Marina had talked. There was a grief, however different, that they shared. But maybe it was more that Marina brought her back to her youth, in a way, to a time that was wonderful and terrible in its instability, while Kat kept her in the present.

Kat and Lu and Oliver and this park: an ongoing present, a stasis that ran counter to the flow of Justine's previous experience of this city, that it was full of ghosts, full of the past. Of streets followed, subways taken. There seemed to be no room for the past now, and Justine wondered if that was because she was a mother to a young child, who didn't yet have a conscious memory. And because she was subject to so many demands on her time and attention. And was this pushing out of the past, this taking-up-all-the-space present, what compelled her to crash the memorial service for James?

Her loss of the past, of James, was a loss, in some ineffable way—minor, maybe, but irrefutable—of the future. There'd been the idea, in the back of her mind, that one day she would see him again, and who would he be and who would she be when that happened? Those irreplaceable people who know your youth. There was always the chance . . . always the chance . . . and now there wasn't.

"Kat," she said.

Kat looked up to reply but was almost immediately distracted by Lu, just as Justine herself had to spot her son as he climbed up a red metal apparatus. By the time Kat asked her what she was going to say, it no longer seemed worth bringing up. She was experiencing a sensation, a breeze, or a scent, not a subject of conversation.

MARINA MET RAFAEL at a restaurant in the shadow of the Williamsburg Bridge. The idea: they'd have a meal and conversation in a geographically neutral place—not within blocks of either of their homes—before they had sex again. It wasn't propriety, but the notion, never said out loud by either of them, that they should "get to know each other." That there was, or ought to be, more than just sex between them. Though "just sex"—that construction, that turn of phrase didn't strike her as right. Was it ever just sex? Even if it was *only* sex, didn't that imply a lack? An incompletion, and therefore not a justness—something remained unaccounted for. She could still return to that afternoon in his apartment in an almost haptic way, his touch on her body, how they had laughed into each other. But even in the amount of time between then and now, a layer of distance had formed. This distance wasn't the former distance they had around each other in the presence of James. There had been a clarity to sex with Rafael, immediately after, which had since been made fuzzy, and she wanted that clarity back. She was waiting for it to return.

There was a doubling, she thought, sitting in a booth by the large window of the converted Pullman car that served as the front room of the restaurant. There's you and me sitting here right now. And then there's you and me that day in your apartment. I can't quite get the four of us to make sense.

The restaurant at this time of night was full of diners, all the stools occupied at the bar, people waiting beyond the door.

How young everybody was. The recognition of this left Marina feeling that she no longer was—young—at least not without some qualification. There was (already? how?) a wave of younger people coming up behind her now. It didn't weigh on Rafael, though. He seemed to have a quiet, abiding confidence that enabled him to be anywhere he chose, and she wondered where he derived it from. And could she ever have it, too?

It ignited a sense of aggression within her, that she wanted to push against.

"That freedom t-shirt you have," she said, from across the table—"Do you only wear it at hotels?"

"The shirt? It was a costume. Pretty much. But no, I didn't wear it around town."

"Right."

"It was a *project* . . . I don't know. It's over."

Marina heard irony, doubt, pride, recalcitrance in the way he said project. He lowered his head, in profile, made a small movement of his mouth, not a smirk or a pout, but as if he were mulling something over with himself.

"I don't want to be a joke," he said. "To you."

"You're not," she said, quickly, a suppression of the fluttering and the sting, her reaction to being complimented and reproved at once.

"Like, I'm that guy with the sneakers and the freedom shirt."

"No, I know."

"Anyway, the t-shirt's folded up in the back of a drawer," he said, smiling.

"Freedom dies in darkness," she said.

"It's democracy that dies in darkness."

"Freedom gets forgotten about, then, until it winds up in a rag bag."

"Exactly."

The last time Marina was at this place, an institution of sorts in this overhauled neighborhood, she hadn't noticed how old or young anybody looked, only that she fit. All the new construction and streetscaping hadn't gone up overnight, though it felt to her like it had, like a magic trick. Or as if a gigantic door were hauled open, sunlight flooding into a cavernous dark, and you walk out of the hangar where a film is being made. The last time she'd sat at a table in this room she hadn't yet met James. It had been with a small group of women. Someone's birthday? A celebratory night, in any case. Among the group was Dahlia: the rising literary light. *Among* was wrong though—Dahlia dominated the group, imposed an uneasy energy on them, made them all deferent to her. How did she accomplish this? Marina wondered, in an anthropological way. Eventually it clicked: Dahlia had a self-dramatizing streak, but one that was difficult to criticize because she wrapped her personal problems in an aggrandizing banner of collective politics. Look at all the structural inequalities that deplete and exhaust us, as women. *Look, look!* Yes, yes, Marina thought, I'm looking, I understand these structural inequalities are real and deeply consequential. I'm looking, but what I'm seeing is that you don't really want solidarity, you want attention. And, okay. Who doesn't want attention? But call it what it is, then. And the real problem, as Marina assessed it, was that for Dahlia the attention only flowed one way. Her interest in things, in people—her attention to them—existed only in direct proportion to the attention they would direct, amplified, toward her.

"So, actually the real problem," said Rafael, in deadpan response to what Marina had just regaled him with, "is that this Dahlia woman doesn't pay you enough attention."

"Yes, totally," And then, again, Marina couldn't suppress a smile.

Their food arrived and they kept up their conversation, eating and talking, and when, at one point, Marina, with animated hands, almost knocked her glass of Malbec over, she recalled Holly and the spilled water that day they'd gone for brunch with Alex Greenman. How Holly's whole nervous system had gone on the fritz, only for a moment, but a moment that took her out of her surroundings, out of the present. And maybe Alex Greenman's reaction to Holly's outpouring was concern, a concern that he didn't know what to do with and so it expressed itself as embarrassment.

Here, now, Marina caught her glass before it fully tipped over, though she wondered what Rafael would have done if a scene had been made. She wondered if one day she would find out, if they would continue to go to places together where that opportunity—to be humiliated or to be understood and comforted—existed.

Distracted with these thoughts, she'd been mindlessly running the fingers of her right hand along the inside of her lower left arm, which lay on the table, exposed. She'd worn a shirt whose sleeves draped only to her elbows. Her left hand extended itself, half open, toward Rafael and it wasn't until he reached for it, placing his hand in hers, that she became aware of her movement, her fingers along her arm.

They walked long blocks under the elevated tracks, warm and humid, rain holding off but certainly on the way. Overhead, the Manhattan-bound train rumbled on toward so many other variations of this night. They climbed the stairs, ascending to go forward, deeper into Brooklyn, to the border of Queens, where he lived. She led the way up, his hands on her waist when they reached the platform under a low, dark sky.

Later, in the not yet light early morning, awake in his bed while he slept, she would wonder if her apartment, in a still unspoken concession, was off-limits because James lingered there, in some form.

And after that, when Rafael was up and in the bathroom, and rain was streaking the bedroom window, she reached into her bag for the clean pair of underwear she'd packed and felt something else, a different piece of fabric, which turned out to

be the napkin that Holly had stained with mascara, now stiff
with dried tears. Marina had been carrying the same bag that
day, when she'd stuffed the stolen napkin in and then forgotten about it. She'd take the napkin home, throw it in the
laundry? Maybe she'd carry it over her head this morning,
walking to the subway, to keep the rain off, like a newspaper
in an old movie. She'd thought to bring extra underwear but
not an umbrella. There were already traces of Rafael on her.
Why not traces of Holly, too.

She opened the window when the rain let up, only spitting
now on the sill, which like the scuffed baseboard was thick
with so many layers of white paint. She took in the smell of
rain, and the patch of green overgrown yard below, where
the branches of a tall tree split a fence between buildings. A
city tree she couldn't properly identify because she was a New
Yorker and she didn't have to.

HOLLY COULDN'T SLEEP.

Nights, in general, were troublesome.

She considered reading. She had read books on grief as part of her training. She had read books on grief when her mother and father died in quick succession. She read more books on grief when Lila died. She supposed there were new ones to read now.

She considered watching a show and found herself in her living room, in the dark, the weak but deep blue of early morning coming through the window. Reggie, her cat, stirred and meowed.

Sweet girl, she said. Though Reggie was, in fact, an older cat. Mature. Sweet lady? What are we, Reg?

Television felt intrusive just then, too loud. Instead, she sat at her desk, opened her laptop, a flare of light, and began to write. A letter. But she wasn't sure whom she wanted to address. She got only as far as Dear.

THE CAPSULE-SIZE ELEVATOR rumbled up to the fifth, top floor. It belonged to different times, different places: The mahogany paneling echoed long-gone drama, the linoleum floor signaled a mid-century technocratic efficiency, and the golden light from the ceiling fixture cast a glow over the compartment, snug as a ship's cabin. You pulled a grated door aside along a track to enter through another door into the apartment itself. In all her years of living in this city, all the buildings she'd been in and out of, Marina had never experienced anything like it.

Adam, who let her in, didn't look much like Marina had pictured, because she had pictured James, more or less, and however illogically. Where James's face was broad but angled, Adam's was aquiline and oval. In a black shirt. Black jeans. Graying hair with a swoop to it. Glasses. His long, fine fingers shook her hand and took the flowers she'd bought at the bodega on her way from the train.

Adam, she intuited, belonged to a category of people, about ten to fifteen years older, that sometimes heightened her sensitivity and self-consciousness. It had to do with a ratio of age to accomplishment. She was rarely intimidated by anyone her age or younger. Or anyone old enough to have been her mother or father—no matter how much they had achieved, there was a sense that they were no longer on the pulse, they didn't have to be, and so there was a diminishment of expectation. Which was why Alex Greenman's level of renown hadn't much affected her, why she'd felt little need to impress him the few times she'd met him with James. And no remorse for that day when she and Holly had left crumbs all over his couch.

On a rock by the lake in the park, she and Justine had simply been two women talking. But here was the husband of her new friend. Here was their home, their son, who burst out of a bathroom and down a short hallway, bright eyes, curly fair hair, round rubbery glasses, followed by Justine in a magenta sweatshirt and loose jeans, barefoot. Here, Marina was a bit like a solicitor, intruding on strangers and hoping to interest them in a sales pitch she herself didn't believe in.

Before she knew it, Adam had taken the bodega flowers and placed them in a vase on a long dining table. A dining table! Her parents had a dining table. She didn't expect to find them in the homes of people her age, but then, Justine and Adam weren't her age. Justine picked up Ollie, as she called him, and sat him on her jutted hip, before placing him in his high chair.

"He's almost getting too big for this," she said, as if Marina understood, when Marina understood only that she understood so little about their world. Nothing beyond an outline or a set of clichés. Wedding invitations from friends arrived with increasing frequency, but parenthood, like a dining table, like this specific variety of domesticity, was still far enough out on the horizon—you could see it gathering in the distance, looming, and wonder with some trepidation whether it might find you or whether it might shift course and blow by you completely. She wondered if Justine was going to ask her to hold Oliver and was both relieved and a little disappointed when she didn't.

Adam toasted bagels they'd bought for her visit and poured coffee, while Justine accepted Marina's compliments on her place and her son. Marina couldn't help commenting on the elevator, how "sick" it was and Justine's smile—

amused, tender—undercut the effect she'd been going for in choosing to use that word. It made her conscious of what she'd been trying, somewhat unconsciously, to do: there are words people age out of and their deployment isn't wholly innocent. She'd wanted Justine to feel that difference between them.

"Yeah, it's sick," Justine said. "But getting Ollie in there in the middle of a tantrum? I need extra arms. I need to be an octopus. And it's a pain in the ass with a stroller."

Marina nodded, of course, yeah, of course. Tantrums. Strollers.

"Ollie doesn't love the stroller, either. He just wants to run everywhere now."

Marina nodded again.

"I'm sorry." Justine shook her head. "Like you care about any of this."

"No, it's fine."

"It can get overwhelming, though. Parenting talk."

"Really, it's fine."

Then Marina remembered the gift she'd brought for Oliver, Ollie. A small, soft dragon, more cuddly than fearsome. She brought it out of her bag and with a little urging from Justine—*Can you thank Marina?*—Ollie did so and snuggled the stuffed animal between his cheek and shoulder.

"What do you think its name is?" Justine asked him.

"Maureen," he said. Which was, apparently, how he pronounced Marina. An associative leap of a name.

Adam laughed at something Marina didn't quite understand, even after he explained that it had to do with the sound of the name Maureen. It was similar to Eileen or Irene, who was a woman who used to live in this apartment before them, whom they'd never met but had created a whole backstory around, and whom they would impersonate.

"Well, it's more like we sometimes attempt to inhabit her spirit," said Adam, bringing the food to the table.

Marina got that this was an extended, ongoing bit between Adam and Justine, but in trying to share it with her, they'd only tightened the exclusiveness of it.

"Maureen's gonna go out for a pack a smokes," Adam said, putting on a voice that crossed a film-noir antihero with Katharine Hepburn.

"And then she'll light them herself with her dragon fire breath," said Justine.

Marina laughed out of obligation and nowhere near as fully as Adam and Justine did. Even Ollie laughed along with his parents. And that, admittedly, was lovely to see. It was all so lovely to see. Why had she come here? When could she leave?

Out of the window beyond the dining table, which looked onto a courtyard garden, the crowns of trees rose above the roofline. Their leaves were turning color against the clouded-over sky. Marina thought of a hotel room in the afternoon, on a high floor, spare and clean, light glancing off the window-panes, a wrought iron railing, tangerines on a table, a view of the sea, where they'd gone swimming earlier. A view of James's long, lean back, as he drew the linen curtains closed against the sun. He'd said: We've only been to cold places together. Let's go somewhere warm. So, they did. They had days in brightness and shadow.

"What do you think, Marina?" Adam asked.

"Oh, I'm not sure," she said. *Repeat the question, please. Repeat whatever you said before the question. And maybe even before that.* "I drifted off a little. I'm sorry. You just have a very nice view there."

"You don't have to be sorry," said Justine. "If you want, we can go out on the fire escape in a bit."

"I'd love that," said Marina. "But, please, tell me what you were saying, Adam. What I missed when I zoned out." She leaned in, elbows on the table, hands folded under her chin. *Pay attention, Marina.* It wasn't exactly James's voice in her head—she'd only heard his voice that one time outside the bookstore—but this directive to herself seemed to come from him. *Pay attention.*

When they finished up, Justine took her out on the fire escape. Adam stayed in with Ollie. A soft wind blew through the treetops, and though they didn't need coats just yet, that was on the way. The darkening of fall, the coming on of change. Somber hours.

"Thanks for having me over."

"Thanks for coming."

They stood, not talking for a moment, looking out across the courtyard into the building of apartments identical to this one.

"Did you always know you wanted this?" Marina ventured to break the silence.

"Wanted what?"

"What you have here. A husband, a kid, a mortgage."

"Yes, I always yearned for a mortgage."

Surrender—to Justine's smiling sarcasm—spread across Marina's face.

"But you know what I mean."

"I know what you mean. And, no, I didn't always know."

Marina wondered if Justine might add something almost pandering: "And somedays I still don't." But she didn't.

"I don't know that I want it. But living with James, there was something so all-in and something so halfway about it at the same time. Like, he literally wasn't there, he was traveling so often. And it got to me in this way I never expected."

"I think," said Justine, her hands on the railing, her gaze directed outward, "we all end up compromising in some way. We give things up. And even if you refuse to compromise—if that's even what James was doing—you give something up."

"He gave me up."

"Oh Marina, I didn't mean it like that." Justine turned, her eyes wide with concern.

"No, it's true. Or I gave him up. Depending on how you look at it."

She'd worried, earlier at the dining table, that she and Justine had lost what they'd had on that rock in Central Park. But it was coming back, on the fire escape and as Justine walked with her to the subway.

The long blocks of historic apartment buildings, their neo-classical columns, their brass plaques, and closer to the train tracks, newer, boxy constructions, you saw them everywhere now. You might be anywhere, or nowhere.

Marina brought up going to Vermont with Holly, to scatter James's ashes, a subject that seemed to coincide with the atmosphere, the weather. It would be winter soon enough.

"Vermont?" Justine asked. Marina named the town, the lake. By the house where the Kanes used to live. Where James and Justine had been children.

"You decided to go?"

"Yeah. You know, when Holly asked me if I would go with her, she put it like she wanted me to go for her. So she wouldn't have to do it alone." Marina said. "And I want to know if you might want to come too? I guess I'm asking the same thing of you."

"Would Holly be okay with it? She doesn't know me."

"I told her you'd been there, to that place, and that could be so helpful, to have you along."

"Okay then. Yes," said Justine, on the sidewalk by the stairs to the elevated 7 train. No hesitation.

Waiting for the train, Marina wondered about Justine's quick decision. How naturally, how easily she'd said yes. Just as naturally as she'd offered her number to Marina at the memorial. As naturally as Marina had accepted it. How Justine reached for Marina. How each of them reached for the other.

That evening, safely returned to her apartment, Marina took her laptop over to her bed. She opened a document, a story, she hadn't touched in months. She deleted most of it and began again, working into the night.

She slept for a few hours and woke up wired, her concentration scattered and in need of a focal point. She had a Sunday ahead of her in which she could do something she'd been meaning to. James had told her about a photo of Holly, the one Alex Greenman took. They'd planned to go see it together at some point, but no urgency had ever made that happen.

She took the train to the museum where it lived as part of the permanent collection. In a modern photography room, one other patron passed by during the time she stood there, but nobody intruded on Marina's view.

She wouldn't have recognized it, she didn't think, as the woman she knew. Maybe because it wasn't exactly a portrait and Holly's face wasn't the primary element. But the more Marina looked at the woman, the way she held herself in the light, by the tall window, the way a calmness met with an uncertainty, vulnerability with confidence, the assuredness of the whole thing—as if it were inevitable and always existed—the more familiar it seemed to her. The space inside the picture, too, because she'd been there, Alex Greenman's loft.

"Is it weird?" Marina had asked James when he'd first mentioned the photograph to her. "Seeing your aunt. Naked."

"Kind of, yeah," he'd admitted. "I didn't buy the postcard version or anything."

They both laughed, an acknowledgment as well as a preemptive closing of the subject on what exactly was weird about James seeing naked young Holly posing for Alex. There wasn't anything explicitly sexual about the image and yet it was hardly a purely formal study. You couldn't abstract the sex from it. You didn't necessarily imagine the photographer and the subject getting it on, but sex was so ambient in it. And so, too, what went with sex, the undercurrents that surfaced, the conscious and unconscious desires.

Your aunt! Marina thought for an instant. And then she ceased to see Holly in relation to James. She saw a woman both in a moment and out of one. And she, too, was in a moment and out of one, standing there in a quiet, not much visited room.

Because she'd paid admission, she figured she should walk around and take in other galleries. And she did, half-engaged, before returning to Holly as if in orbit.

For all the interest she took in the photograph aesthetically, what drew her back and kept her there was a kind of self-interest. That Holly—this image-Holly and the real one—had something to impart to her about her own life. Who she was, who she wanted to be. Information that seemed to contrast with other information she'd been taking in, that contrasted with Justine's information. And then she wanted Justine to see this photograph and to witness what Justine would make of it.

Marina hadn't stayed up into that early morning, writing, with Holly in mind. She wasn't writing *for* Holly, but the expectation that Holly would read what she had written couldn't be extracted from Marina's motivation. And, too, the sense that whatever she was writing was an element of a larger, ongoing conversation she and Holly were carrying on, had started carrying on when James died, even when they weren't in active communication. She wasn't nearly ready to send anything to Holly yet. But returning home from the museum, she went to her bed, brought up Holly's number in her phone, and called.

Holly answered. Yes, she could talk. No, it wasn't a bad time. She was happy to hear from Marina. Assuming nothing was wrong?

"Nothing's wrong," said Marina. "I mean, nothing new. I hope it's not weird. I just felt like hearing your voice. Like, your actual voice."

There was something similar about Holly's voice and James's. The intonation, the phrasing.

"No, it's nice," said Holly.

Marina told her how she'd gone to see the photograph that Alex Greenman had taken.

"You did," said Holly. She had that way of saying something that wasn't exactly a question but wasn't entirely a neutral statement either. It was leading, it required a response. Not necessarily a justification—Holly's tone didn't sound angry or defensive, just curious and a little wary.

"It's so alive, Holly. I just. I don't know. I thought it would, like, *tell* me something. Like that abstract painting we were talking about, the one on the wall at Alex Greenman's. That it would affect me in that same way."

"And did it?"

"Yes. And it made me wonder."

"About what?"

"A lot of things." How to put it? In the gallery at the museum, Marina had grown irritated at the fact that this beautiful photograph of Holly hung on the wall of an institution, where even if Holly's name appeared in the curatorial box of text next to the frame, it meant nothing to most people. Holly was aesthetic marginalia. A footnote. And maybe her name shouldn't mean much to people. Maybe that wasn't the point. But what riled Marina, on Holly's behalf—and on her own behalf?—was that the world looked at the photograph and credited Alex Greenman, as though Alex had made her beautiful when it was Holly who created beauty in the work.

She didn't yet know how to say that to Holly. So, instead:

"Does it seem like a long time ago to you? Like something you've moved on from, even though it's continually new, in a way. To a new viewer, I mean."

"It probably feels that way to Alex, as a photographer. It's his early work. To me, it's both. It's a long time and it's no time. I don't know if you can really understand that until you get to be a certain age."

"But with Alex Greenman—you're still close, obviously. And . . . well . . . I have to say I kind of got angry, standing there, looking at the picture. Angry at the circumstances surrounding it all."

"I've gotten angry, too." Holly sighed. "But Alex, you know, he's like family at this point. And I need whatever family I can get. I'm the last of my line, Marina. It ends with me." Holly laughed a little, but Marina didn't.

"Holly."

"I don't want to sound flip. I'm sorry."

"No."

"I just can't get the enormity of it into words."

They fell into silence, which Marina eventually felt obligated to break, and then apologize for breaking, as if it were a weakness. As if Holly had achieved a monk-like mastery of quietude she could only aspire to.

"Well, I went to see your picture because of something I can't fully articulate either."

"What should we talk about then? There's got to be something we can put into language." Her laugh again.

"I don't know." Marina heard meowing on the line. "Is that your cat?"

"Yeah, that's Reggie. My sweet girl."

"How is she doing?"

"Well, she's still alive."

"Holly." Marina's voice had laughter in it now, but also a note of pleading.

"I'm sorry, Marina. I can't seem to help myself. Tell me something else. Tell me something about you."

HOLLY HAD A PATIENT, a man named Carl, who lived a floor below a woman with heavy footfalls. Carl called his upstairs neighbor Sasquatch and silently seethed when she walked above his head. She wasn't even very large—there was simply something about her gait and the way her feet hit the floorboards, and whatever lay between those boards and Carl's ceiling, resulting in an acoustic amplification. Carl's girlfriend, Jenny, wasn't nearly as bothered by the thudding. So, Carl was on his own, both in his predicament and in trying to resolve it. Not uncommon for him. He had a difficult time speaking directly to Sasquatch—who happened to be a lovely, pleasant person—about the problem, and while this inability to confront the situation wasn't the reason he was seeing Holly, it was emblematic of the deeper work they'd been doing over the past couple of years, involving patterns developed in Carl's childhood, behaviors his parents had shaped, consciously or not. Now that Jenny was pregnant, those patterns took on new resonance and much of their session time was lately spent discussing Carl's concerns about fatherhood. Though Jenny and Carl had wanted this pregnancy, he was understandably nervous. What was the right amount of nervous to be? he'd asked, sitting in a club chair in Holly's office. (He always went for the chair, never the couch). Despite his concerns, there was, however, one aspect he wasn't worried about—was even positively anticipating, in fact, though his positivity itself troubled him. This was: not having to care how loud and disturbing their baby might be, in the middle of the night or on a quiet weekend afternoon, and whether the noise carried. The noise would be retributive. Sasquatch payback. She would have to live with it as he had to live with her heavy steps.

"What kind of parent am I going to be," he asked Holly, "if that's what I'm thinking about? In those terms?"

"Which terms, exactly?" Holly said.

"That I'm already conceiving of my child as a prop. For my own trivial, ridiculous purposes. For retaliation."

She tried to reassure him. With Carl, she often had the impression that what he was telling her he'd already said at a party, socially, for a laugh, and that he was repeating it to her to get at the gravity that nevertheless remained, the splinter of anguish at the heart of a joke. Sometimes she wished she were at that party, with a drink, despite her genuine desire and professional duty to improve his mental health.

The undercurrent of Carl's therapy they repeatedly delved into had to do with a certain sadness. Sadness that Carl hadn't been mothered well. Sadness for the child he'd been and sadness, too, for his mother. He didn't want that particular sadness for his child, how heavy it had been and still, at times, was.

"Parenting and being parented, it's a bit of a rigged game," Holly said. "It's something of a setup, there's no real way to win." It sounded good, epigrammatic. He seemed to take it as insight.

But, she added, winning and losing was not the most helpful way to look at it, and already she was tired of the gaming metaphor she'd trotted out. She really wanted to say, "Jesus fucking Christ, Carl, you're having a child. You're bringing life into the world! Be happy about it for five fucking minutes!" Professional restraint kept her poker-faced.

"Because even if you win, you lose?" Carl took it up, but before she could respond in any substantive way, their session had come to an end. They'd continue next week.

That evening, at home, she thought of Carl and cringed a

little at the outburst she'd only had in her head. Carl took his feelings seriously, and it was on her to take those feelings seriously enough to help him examine them. Even those feelings he had toward Sasquatch. To treat Carl's feelings as trivial would be to treat her own work as trivial and it wasn't. Her work had sustained her, was sustaining her now, especially.

Holly tried to imagine Carl's girlfriend, Jenny. She'd heard a lot about her, most of it positive. According to Carl, their relationship wasn't the issue, they were a good fit. They communicated well, listened to each other. But did Jenny hear the farcical party version of Carl's experiences and his reaction to events or did she get the after-party comedown version, the version that hurt? Both, probably, Holly figured. You needed both if you were ever going to get anywhere with another person. As Carl had said in previous sessions, Jenny wasn't unduly bothered by the sound of the footsteps upstairs, but she didn't entirely disregard Carl's sensitivity.

Holly was thinking aloud, but talking to whom? Not to her cat, Reggie. She was talking, she realized, to the urn of James's ashes that now sat on the desk in her living room, like a plant or a pile of bills. She was telling the ashes about Carl and Jenny and Sasquatch.

Sometimes she forgot the urn was there until she remembered she had a responsibility toward it, the way you remember to water a plant or pay a bill. She didn't think of it as James, though she spoke to it, at it, instead of speaking to the air. How to put it: she wasn't entirely alone in the room. There was some friendly energy around her. It reminded her of the slinky black cat she and James had bought as a joke at the hospital gift shop for Lila, who had kept it by her bed and named it Mona. Even now, Holly thought: *Mona?* Mona.

She would have to scatter the ashes, in keeping with James's wishes. But then who or what would she talk to? Mona the cat was probably packed away in a box marked: LILA. It would take work to find it, and then, she didn't really want a weirdly sexy stuffed cat sitting on her desk. She didn't go for kitsch, decoratively. Especially not deathbed kitsch. But the Lila box, wherever it was, deep in a closet—it only occurred to her just then that she had been saving that box for James. And now? You go to thrift stores or flea markets and see old photographs of people, with inscriptions on the back, and you wonder how those pictures got there, who would have given such things away? You give them away when there's no one left to save them for. Who would ever know the history of Mona the cat? It would die and disappear with Holly herself.

As she'd told Marina, she was the only one left.

As she'd also told Marina, Alex was family. To be relied upon as family. Always in each other's lives. (They were *mischpacha* he might say, with only a hint of irony at his use of Yiddish, an expression of his father. How Jewish of him.) That was a conversational answer, though. Not a lie, but not a belief of which Holly was thoroughly convinced. The reality of it dissolved if you looked too closely. Perhaps because Alex didn't exactly need to rely on her. He had Susan. He had his art and his reputation. And he'd never sustained a loss as great as Holly's. Or as multiform. Suffering one loss, she had learned, didn't make suffering another particularly easier. When she put it to herself that way, it sounded like a competition. (The one competition she could handily win.) But it wasn't really a question of magnitude.

Alex didn't fully understand what she was going through, or didn't want to. She thought of him now in relation to Marina. Look at Marina—who couldn't possibly understand what Holly was going through but who was the only one with whom . . . with whom . . . with whom what? Holly got stuck there for a minute.

With whom she found she could talk—about James, or not about James—and have it generate something other than a sad, platitudinous empathy. Marina's comprehension, not of what Holly was going through, necessarily, but of who Holly was.

Thank you for her, she said to the ashes.

MARINA LOVED TO DRIVE, maybe because she was late to learn. Growing up in Manhattan, she'd never had to. It wasn't until college—California—that she'd gotten her license. Marina was happy to drive the whole way to Holly's, she said, and Justine was happy to let her, to simply sit there and drift. The times she was away from her son for more than a day were rare. And this lightness, this abandon, having to account only for oneself, was a kind of freedom. She thought back to Marina momentarily losing focus at their dining table. She thought of Rafael and his t-shirt.

"Why?" Adam had asked, about this trip, in a tone more reflective than upset or concerned. Why did she want to go? Because Marina had asked her to and going would be an act of friendship. True enough. And it was time away. A break she knew she could get—Adam wouldn't or couldn't object, not when they ultimately all depended on her, financially, for the roof over their heads. His ethically unimpeachable, fulfilling nonprofit work didn't pay the bills. *From each according to his ability, to each according to his needs*—she subscribed to that in theory, in dinner party conversation, and even at the voting booth. But she could never quite relinquish the practical, middle-class, individualistic ethos she'd been raised with, that instilled the value of, and drew security from, backup plans and rainy-day funds. Which gave her a double measure of power, if she should ever need to exercise it, within her own little family: economic stability and personal martyrdom.

Look how I've made this compromise and sacrifice—of my time and myself—for you, my loves.

She never exercised this power, but she knew she could. Compromise, sacrifice. What she and Adam were doing, incrementally, every day. And yet her life with Adam and Oliver didn't really feel like a compromise or a sacrifice. Most of the time. It felt like a choice, a good choice she had made. A choice she was proud of. How could you not value the ability to choose? She did. She did! But there was responsibility in choosing, a gravity in it. And for the moment, for this long weekend, she would be happy to cede responsibility to Marina.

So, in answer to Adam's question—which she hadn't really answered at the time he'd asked her, hadn't known exactly how to answer—it was friendship, it was a kind of vacation, yes. But it was also this: she hadn't shaken James's death. It wasn't that she missed him, that his absence appreciably altered the pattern of her days. It was a larger, more existential sense of being repeatedly brought up short, countered by moments of an almost cosmic sense of belonging. Belonging? To what or to whom? Marina? And by extension to Holly? How quickly she'd said yes when Marina told her that James wanted his ashes scattered at the lake by the Kanes' house.

Marina seemed pleased to have the responsibility, the control. It was a return to form, Justine thought, a return to her first impression of Marina as quietly take-charge, a little forward, coming up and speaking to her at the memorial. Though this return didn't so much confirm Justine's understanding of Marina's personality as underscore the extent to which personality, or its effects, could be contextual. When Marina had come over to Justine's place, when she'd met Adam and Ollie, Marina had shrunk. Her lack of presence, of confidence, created an empty space into which went Justine's competent superiority. It wasn't triumphant; if anything, Justine tried to make her actions look like hospitality and inclusion, but their family life had subdued Marina. A framework into which she didn't fit.

In the interval between then and now, she and Marina had met up one weekend afternoon when Marina took her to see the photo of Holly. She continued to experience a mix of emotions upon hearing from Marina, getting a text or a message, and then seeing her. Some excitement, some slight unrest. But the overarching feeling was consolation for a loss she didn't quite know she had.

Going to the museum to see the photo of Holly had been a thing to do, like going to a movie or going out to lunch. Nothing as strong as obsession propelled them there, though maybe there was more fascination on Marina's part. Justine had been surprised by Marina's proprietary affect: a sense that Holly belonged to Marina and that Marina was being generous, letting her in on it.

"It's beautiful," Justine had said as they stood in the quiet room. She'd seen a lot of Alex Greenman's work, though, leafed through thick books of his that Adam had bought, and this photograph wasn't, to her eyes, necessarily his strongest. Which was maybe a commentary on just how strong his whole body of work was. Because this image really was beautiful. But Marina seemed to want something more from Justine.

"Does it remind you of James?" Justine added, trying to guess at what that something more might be.

"No," said Marina. "Well, maybe just a little. There is some resemblance in her face. I don't know, I just want to keep coming back to it."

Justine had the impression that Marina was slightly disappointed in her. Perhaps if she knew Holly, had spent some time with her the way Marina had she would have had a stronger reaction, more in tune with Marina's . . .

She would have that chance now.

At the wheel, Marina didn't shrink as she had that day at Justine's. Nor did she seem a little let down. They were, once again, two women. Once on a rock in a park, now behind the windshield of a car. Soon enough, they would be three.

Justine looked out the window, at the early January trees stripped of leaves, out beyond the Hutchinson River Parkway. It was always something of an escape to leave New York, requiring the mentality of departure. She thought of Greyhound buses, New England–bound. Driving up the West Side, through the Bronx. In the summer. Full sun on the streets, hot concrete, large brick buildings for blocks and blocks, double-hung windows framed in black aluminum, a curtain or a flag tacked up. A strange sense of stillness within movement, of the bus, of the city itself.

By early afternoon, they pulled onto the street where Holly lived. Neither Marina nor Justine knew this neighborhood near Boston. Somerville, where tall, old houses sat close to the sidewalk, some spruced up, others in disrepair. Holly, with her weekender, a bag of groceries, and the ashes, stood on the porch of a robin's egg blue Victorian that had been divided into condos. Justine thought of the woman in Alex Greenman's photograph, and then she remembered the slightly drawn but still self-possessed woman Marina had pointed out at the memorial. She remembered Holly's dignity.

Now, beneath an army-green parka and black hat, Holly looked less troubled, but her manner still quietly commanded you to take her seriously. It wasn't formality but a way of carrying herself, an understanding of her body, the dancer she had been, maybe. And this, along with the fact that her familial bond to James outweighed Justine's whatever-it-was connection made Justine offer to take the back seat so Holly could have the front. Holly's acceptance established a hierarchy, but not an oppressive one. Justine felt large-hearted, not diminished, in acquiescing to it, in occupying her inferior place.

"Where should I put James?" Holly asked, settling into the front seat, with the ashes on her lap. "If that's not too crass."

"He could go in back?" Marina suggested. "If you're okay with that, Justine?"

"Oh yeah, of course," Justine replied, wondering, in the ever-alert way of a parent of a young child, how attentive she might have to be. Was this container leak-proof? Was there a risk of him spilling? Justine settled the urn snugly between two bags on the seat next to her. She could keep an eye on it—him?—but could also look away.

Justine and Holly had never formally been introduced until now. They made small talk, for a bit, but small talk as a co-operative effort that was acknowledged and rewarded with an incrementally greater level of ease with each other.

Justine anticipated that Marina's manner might change once Holly joined them, in the way that Marina had made herself smaller around Justine's husband and child. But then, Holly wasn't a husband nor was she a child. And Marina's manner remained the same.

Holly struck Justine as the kind of person she herself used to be, perhaps an older version, a person whose unattachment made her lonely. A person whose loneliness made her unattached. She hadn't seen that loneliness in Alex Greenman's photograph of her. Maybe it was there, though, and she hadn't noticed it. Maybe that's what Marina had wanted her to see. Holly's loneliness, Justine surmised, wasn't as desperate as hers had once been. It didn't grab onto people, it was much more comfortable with itself, less aggressive. But Justine still recognized it. Marina had obviously told Holly about Justine, the tenuous extent of her connection to James—a day spent with him as a child, a night spent with him later. That tenuousness had apparently been enough for Holly.

If they didn't make many stops, it would take just under three hours. They drove past dirty banks of snow, toward gray bands of sky, but inside the car they didn't feel cold. It would be dark by the time they got to the house Holly had booked for the weekend, but not too late at night.

Holly was saying she didn't know what, exactly, it was about this place that held such meaning for James. Only that he'd spent time there as a child. A time that was out-of-time, she imagined. A break with your usual life and routines. A re-orienting. Time with a family that must have made him consider his own family in relation, how different they were and what difference could mean.

"The Kanes," said Holly. "Well, you knew them," she added, turning back to face Justine. "When Marina told me that, I thought, of course she should join us."

Why the Kanes' house? Of all the places he'd traveled to, everywhere he'd lived—why did that place call him back? Justine wasn't so self-centered to think it had much to do with her, but that weekend they'd spent there as children was also burned into her memory. It was hardly the only getaway her parents had ever taken her on. The families, the Kanes and the Manns, weren't such great friends, they didn't see each other all that often and lived in different towns. And what, even, was the connection again? Some professional tie between the fathers. Their parents would go out for dinner and perhaps see each other at parties and Ted or Helena must have said: Let's get the kids together. Come to our country place! But the Manns had traveled farther, seen other sights, other people, other cultures. And still. That weekend had irrevocably shaped her. It had to do with sex. Ted Kane's hand on Helena Kane's waist, between her jeans and sweater. James above her on the bed. If James hadn't been there, to give form and direction to whatever it was that Ted's hand on Helena's waist had made her feel, would the image, the memory have taken shape and taken hold in her mind? And wasn't that what

James did? What he'd done? With his photographs: turn moments into images that took hold of one's mind?

"He told me once what it was about this place," said Marina, from the front. That being there had been his first conscious experience of a certain freedom, she explained. If Justine heard a faint note of irony in Marina's use of the word, a reference to Rafael's t-shirt, Holly didn't seem to. "Like, a feeling of accession and expansion," Marina continued. "And he told me about the Kanes. He was talking about his mom, and we didn't talk about her a lot, but he was telling me how the Kanes had this suspicion of her and fascination with her and then also this need for him. To make their family work."

"I would pick up James from their house sometimes," said Holly. "Not their Vermont house, the one in Boston, in the suburbs. It was a big house, but carpeted and cozy, and there was always this golden light coming from the front windows because I would pick him up in the evenings, in winter. There was a year there where I must have been by half a dozen times, after school. Helena, the wife, was beautiful. And efficient. Very good at sizing other people up, in relation to her own needs. She sized up Lila to be a bit of a threat."

"How did she size up you?" asked Marina.

"I think I was just there. I was a mode of transportation for James."

That aligned with Justine's memory of Helena Kane. Her ski sweater and slim jeans, her long, falling-apart braid. Her canny look of experience.

"And Ted," Holly continued, "the husband, he had this real New England patrician look. Sporty but smart, like he could chop wood and rig a sailboat and also knew his way around a cocktail. I don't know if he really did any of those things, but he gave off that impression. And like he knew it, too. Like I was supposed to be impressed by it. If not impressed, then aware of it as a thing. And I was. But I didn't necessarily find it attractive. It was a throwback, even then, an affectation. Which is to say, he wasn't my type."

"Was he Lila's type?" Justine asked.

"No, not at all. Except maybe that made him her type."

As Marina drove them down the highway, Holly explained, in the almost clinical psychological vein she'd established, that an element of degradation had been mixed into the alloy of Lila's desire. Not necessarily sexually, as far as Holly knew. But emotionally, to the extent you could separate the two. And it wasn't even that Lila was drawn to men who degraded her. She was attracted to situations in which she had to degrade herself. Lower herself. These competing impulses in Lila, the toggle between degradation and superiority, not so much a contradiction as two sides of one coin. But the degradation: James's father. Michael. Holly had liked him, she did, but she could never forgive him for leaving—not even leaving Lila, that happens, but leaving his son. He never came calling, either, not even once James began to build a reputation, when an opportunist would have crawled out of the woodwork. But that had never been Michael's game. Perhaps he simply didn't know about James's success, couldn't let himself know. She supposed it was deep shame that kept him away.

Justine looked over to the ashes, which sat securely next to her, and she felt protective of them, as if they were to be guarded. They weren't James, though. They were an emanation of him? She'd been kidding with herself before, about the vessel being spill-proof, if she ought to buckle it in, but how awful and pathetic would it be if the urn jerked forward and his dust flew into the grooves of the floor mat, mixed with the residue of road salt and snow? Followed by having to stop the car, collect and shake the contaminated soot back into the urn, and then drive on.

Holly continued: Lila was younger, by about ten years, than most of the parents with kids James's age. Those parents treated her as though she had emigrated from a country with a pitiably low standard of living, and while she spoke the language well enough, she didn't yet know the codes that everyone operated under and didn't have the means to share their concerns. She was condescended to, sometimes offered help and understanding, and on rare occasions, sought out and admired for her difference. Though at those times it was hard for her not to feel like a bit of a mascot. Most of the people in that town lived in stately houses with front lawns and backyards and Lila raised James in a small apartment, left a larger apartment for a smaller one where the schools were better.

"I don't think," Holly said, "there was ever anything between Lila and Ted Kane beyond weird, charged vibes. But I don't know, maybe there was more. She never told me. And I didn't ask. There were weekends I would take James, to spend time with him and help her out. It's possible she could have spent that time with Ted Kane, or someone like him. Maybe he even took her to the house on the lake, if his family wasn't there."

They let this suggestion hang in the air.

And then, there were weekends when the Kanes let Lila and James have the Vermont house to themselves, weekends when the Kanes weren't using it, Holly said.

Justine could see them: James at thirteen, fourteen, and Lila, who must have resembled Holly in Alex Greenman's photograph. Mother and son. She could picture Lila looking at James while he was unaware, walking into or out of the water, lying in the sun or inside on the couch. It was how she looked at Oliver as he slept.

They made good time and were quick about stops. At a rest area in New Hampshire, disinfectant stung Marina's airways as she stood washing her hands next to a large woman with a saggy face and clipped gray hair. The woman's hooded green sweatshirt had a Celtics logo across the front—a leprechaun in a clover-covered waistcoat and hat, wearing pilgrim shoes, smoking a pipe, and spinning a basketball with one hand while leaning on a cane with the other. There was a lot going on there, it seemed to Marina, who had only ever had a passing interest in professional team sports. This woman, she thought, was one of Rafael's women, his hotel breakfast women. But there wasn't any aggression coming off her, and her face wasn't mean and judgmental so much as preoccupied, distracted. When the woman couldn't get the automatic soap dispenser to work, she came back into herself once again, into the moment, and smiled at Marina.

"Fucking technology." She laughed.

"Yeah," Marina said, laughing back. "Fuck that shit."

The woman moved, while humming quietly, to the dispenser one sink down, which was operating properly, and asked Marina if she'd had a good day and told Marina her own day had been okay. And when she said, "All right, take it easy, honey," as they made their way out of the bathroom and parted in the food court, the term of endearment genuinely buoyed Marina.

She reached for her phone to text Rafael, but thought better of it. Why ruin the fellow feeling? Turning the woman into one of his women. She might call him, later that weekend. They would definitely text at some point. He knew where she was and with whom and why. He hadn't asked to come along, even though he'd been close to James. Somehow, somewhere along the line, it had been established that Holly and Marina and Justine formed a trio, three women, charged with carrying out this ceremonial task. Without getting too mythical about it, Marina had the sense that she was operating in the depths of ritual as she got back in the car, under the glare of the lights in the now dark parking lot of the rest stop.

Holly's phone lit up with a text from her neighbor: *Key works fine. Reggie all good. Kept dinner down.* Receiving news of her pet from Sarah, one half of the couple who had recently moved into the condo that occupied one third of the old house Holly lived in, made her feel like an aging woman who receives texts about her aging cat from young people. Their solicitousness toward her wasn't patronizing but nevertheless had a subtle, bitter flavor. They were nice people, she liked them! But their kindness seemed to come with an ulterior motive they could never quite disguise. They were the sort of newcomers who got accused of pricing out the people of Holly's socioeconomic status from certain neighborhoods. Caring for Reggie, effusively saying hello to Holly, offering her a bottle of wine or some treat they had baked, absolved them of any guilt, proved that they were community-minded, that they were *good*. Was Holly being cruel? Petty? There they were, taking care of Reggie out of neighborliness. She wasn't really going to be put out. If the implication of it all bothered her, it wasn't the fault of Sarah and Everett. She *was* an aging woman now who received texts from young people about her aging cat.

When she herself was about Sarah and Everett's age, she wasn't married and living in a condo. She was renting that apartment with the cheap carpeting over the concrete floors where she could give dance lessons. James came to stay with her often, then. Weekends when Lila could be alone, or not alone, but not with James. Holly hadn't loved that place initially, but she grew to love the associations of it, and so she looked back on it with love. James, when he was a boy, lying on the couch, her old cat Millie at his feet, a black-and-white lump of fur and heat.

And in those days, before James went to bed, Holly had to give him a dose of a drug his pediatrician prescribed for his eczema. (He must have inherited the skin condition from his father, and like Michael, it too later disappeared.) The inflammation was mostly on the insides of his elbows and in the hollows of his knees—what James called his "leg pits." He didn't seem to mind the syrup he had to swallow; he seemed to see the taking of it as something special that distinguished him. The syrup, Holly remembered, was called Atarax. Who had come up with that brand name? She knew the word they must have derived it from: ataraxia. It meant the absence of disturbance. She once went out with someone who was pursuing a doctorate in classics, who knew ancient Greek. It took her a minute to recall his name. Glenn? Glenn. She couldn't come up with a surname. So many names and surnames now in her past. So many details from other people's lives—too many details—in her consciousness. Ataraxia, the word and its meaning, came to her though. And an image of eight-year-old James, free from disturbance, drifting into sleep.

After dinner at a restaurant in town, they drove out of well-lit streets and into the pitch dark of back roads illuminated only by the headlights of their car, Marina at the wheel and Holly navigating from her phone. Slowing along the paved road, looking for the dirt turnoff that led down to the houses around the lake. Of the three of them, only Justine had been here before. In the dark. It was familiar in the way of a repeated dream, not a recurring one, but one that even as you're dreaming you recognize, on some sleep-enveloped level, you've had a variation of before.

The steep road down would have been treacherous in the snow and ice in the wrong kind of car, with the wrong kind of wheels. Which was the kind of car they had, so they were lucky that the road itself was clear enough, snow banked on the shoulders and at the feet of the tall trees they wound down through. Holly might have been thinking along the same lines as Justine when she said the owner of the house had informed her that while the lake was frozen, the cold didn't last nearly as long as it had in the past.

"James didn't really have to travel around the world to document climate change," Marina said. "He could have just come here." No bitterness in her voice. More like bewilderment. As if it all could have gone differently and no differently at all.

At the bottom of the hill, one small house and then another came into view, neither of them lit, no vehicles in the drives. Further on, they encountered signs of people, a glow in the windows of the houses by the place they pulled into. It wasn't the house that had belonged to the Kanes, with the red door and the metal roof. This one had a more rustic look. Less Helena, less efficiently beautiful.

They turned off the car, trudged into the house, almost forgot James in the back seat, before Justine went back out to get him.

"Sorry," she said to the ashes, to the air, to whoever might be listening in whatever form.

In the morning, cold and fresh, after she'd put on the coffee that Holly brought and before anyone else was up, Justine pulled on her boots and coat and went walking, trying to locate the Kanes' house from memory. But either she remembered the house wrong or it had been torn down and replaced. She was the only one about so early in the morning and she couldn't recall the last time she'd been alone like this, not another person, not even a stranger, in sight. Certainly not since Oliver had been born. She could recall being lonely—not the desperate, grasping loneliness of her youth, the loneliness that had said yes to James, but the loneliness that new motherhood could surround you with. In that loneliness, though, there were always other people: Adam, Oliver, Kat, Lu, other children, other mothers, friends, coworkers, people on the subway, in shops, on the street. She could not recall being alone. There was no epiphany to have just now, no profundity to grasp—by the frozen lake itself, at the back of the house where they were staying—only a sense of unreality, of fourth dimensionality, of having stepped out of time, as Holly had put it earlier when talking about James. And the thought that if she hadn't said yes to James, if her old loneliness hadn't propelled her toward him, for as briefly as it did, she wouldn't be standing there under a silent, white sky.

The house was gone, James was gone, and she was standing here as someone new. She'd been someone new for a while now. No epiphany, only time and change.

If she hadn't initially understood why she'd crashed the memorial service for James, hadn't understood the murky dissatisfaction that had compelled her to turn up at Alex Greenman's loft, she knew what she was doing here. She had gotten in the car and arrived at this spot in service to Marina and Holly and she would give them what they needed and they would give her what she needed, and then she would go back to Adam and Oliver and she would give them what they needed and they would give her what she needed. Which wasn't resolution. What they would give her was the antidote, the only antidote, as far as she knew, to precarity.

The winter sun was burning off the clouds, the sky becoming bluer through the windows by the table where Justine and Holly sat with coffee, plates of toast and eggs. The rental was clean and well-ordered, but the kitchen décor hadn't been updated for years. Wood cabinets with tarnished chrome pulls, a dull Formica countertop, blue-green checkerboard linoleum floor. A weary fridge. The heat worked well, warming the pine floors throughout the rest of the house, and they'd slept soundly enough. Marina especially, after all that driving. Still, she'd woken up sluggish and irritable, with no specific cause to pin it on. Something less than a complete awareness tugged at her, so that she wasn't entirely sure what was doing the tugging, only that she wanted to kick it away. On top of whatever it was, she was annoyed, too, about the fact that she had an expectation to meet; that Holly and Justine were there and she would need to make an effort not to be peevish.

However vaguely, she began to connect her fractiousness with subjects of conversation brought up the day before, on the drive. James and his mother Lila, the talk of the Kanes. Why that should leave her in this mood she couldn't explain. It hadn't upset her at the time. But now, being here, in this place, the lake, that had belonged, as belonging goes, to James, a shadow of indignation fell on her. No one had forced her to come here. Holly, yes, had appealed to her—*please, for my sake,* the same way Marina had appealed to Justine—but Holly hadn't pressured her and it wasn't Holly who aggravated her, not really. No, it was James himself. That he had put her in this position, made her grieve and made her feel that she didn't entirely know who and what she was really grieving, and by extension, that she was grieving wrong. That she had broken up with him and then he had gone off and died like that.

She pulled on a thick sweater and met Holly and Justine already sitting at the table. They looked up at her invitingly and she figured she was concealing her sourness well enough.

"Where's James?" she asked, almost as a challenge to herself, to see if she could sustain the performance without breaking face. But she also couldn't help herself, bringing up the source of her irritation, like repeatedly feeling for a cut in your mouth. Holly pointed to a side table next to the sofa where the urn sat by a couple of local guidebooks.

"Are you all right?" Holly asked.

"I'm fine," she answered. "I just . . ." She did a kind of shrug-wince.

"It's okay," said Holly. "It's a weird thing, being here."

"Yeah."

"It is beautiful here, though," said Justine. "Weirdness aside."

Marina couldn't argue with that. The curtains had been

pulled from the glass doors at the end of the room that faced the lake, the snow, the rising trees, and the sky.

"It reminds me of a trip I took with James one winter," Marina said. "To the mountains. We went hiking. Snowshoeing, I mean. It was so fucking cold but so pretty. Glittering snow, tree branches bent with ice, falling water frozen on the rocks. Like walking through a fairytale."

Justine started to say something but stopped.

"What?" asked Marina.

"I think I saw a really great picture of you there." One of the first images she'd seen of Marina, that day she'd read the news about James, frozen in her office chair, scrolling, scrolling, scrolling. "On social media, or something, when James died."

"Oh. Yeah." Marina stirred with that strange mix of flattery and minor excitement, of being paid attention to, and the vague disquiet of not knowing exactly who'd been paying attention, except that you'd solicited that not-knowing by putting it out there for whoever might see. On some level, the not-knowing and the disquiet must have appealed to her.

"You looked happy."

"I was happy." Which was true. But she hadn't been *only* happy.

He'd left her on that trip—a dramatic way to put it, though true. When he'd gone walking without his phone and no real regard for her and whether she might be worried. When she was concerned he would judge her for her concern: that it was too much, unwanted. And more than that, once he'd safely returned and her concern shifted into antagonism and the first suspicion that this wasn't a lapse on his part.

"It's the obvious, cliché thing about those posts," Marina said. "About any picture. Never mind filtering or whatever. You're only getting the representation of one moment, not the before or after. Or even what you were thinking, really."

But immediately Marina thought about the portrait of Holly,

which seemed to represent so much more than the moment it captured. It conjured mystery, glimpses of life lived in that room and life beyond the tall window Holly had stood near.

"What were you thinking? At the time of the picture, in the mountains," asked Holly. "Do you remember?"

Marina wasn't sure if she'd been thinking this at the time, but in retrospect what had been going through her mind that weekend had to do with the line between self-absorption and self-negation. Who had she really been worried for that weekend? James or herself?

"It can be both," said Holly. "Concern for someone else doesn't have to be totally selfless on your part. Maybe it can't be."

"But there's a line, right? A threshold, but it keeps moving and I'm not sure where I stand in relation to it," said Marina. "When something is about you and when it's not. And when that matters."

Associatively, she told them about a friend—was Dahlia really a friend, though?—whom she'd tried to reach out to on a couple of occasions—to congratulate her on a getting a book deal, and then again when the book was published and appreciatively reviewed (though Marina hadn't read the novel and most likely never would). Dahlia, whose face she had seen so prominently displayed in the window of the bookstore she'd passed after leaving Holly at Alex Greenman's. Dahlia who had once held court at a restaurant, urging their table to look—*look*—at the systems that oppressed them, and then "forgot" to put in for the tip. Professionally, Dahlia had accomplished what Marina hadn't yet, but still hoped to. (Yes? She hadn't completely let go and given up?) And so, if anything, that placed Dahlia in a position of superiority, no? Not so much that she wouldn't even deign to respond, but enough to set the terms between them and solidify who was at an advantage. Marina saw no apparent reason why she received no response either time and wondered if Dahlia disliked her and had only behaved warmly toward her when in the presence of mutual friends. No, you're being completely self-absorbed, Marina had reasoned. It's not about you at all, she's either too busy or going through something that's preventing her from getting back to you. Maybe she has social hang-ups, anxieties, fears that you're not aware of. Besides, it's not that important. Your relationship to each other is tangential at best.

"That's probably what it was," said Justine, though it seemed that both Justine and Marina were waiting for Holly to chime in with an overriding verdict. And she did.

"I don't know about that." Holly leaned back in her chair and folded her arms, a posture of skepticism, which drew Marina in.

"I bet it did have to do with you. That something about you makes her insecure. If it was really nothing, she could've responded easily enough. All she had to say was 'Thanks.' At least once. You weren't asking very much of her."

It was vindicating, what Holly said. And Marina loved her for it, the way she'd loved her when Holly had broken down and shattered the glass at that restaurant with Alex Greenman.

"I think she was nominated for a big prize," said Marina. "And now I wonder if I shouldn't send her a congratulatory note just to fuck with her. Like, here you go, all the best, looking forward to your non-reply!"

Justine smiled. The pettiness.

"I already hate this woman," said Holly. "Just from the little you've said. But I don't think she's worth the time and energy."

"You're a therapist, how can you hate her?" asked Marina, laughing.

"My profession doesn't require me to like everybody. Just to listen to them if they pay me. And to try to help."

Marina hadn't thought of Holly as particularly cynical or prickly. And Holly hadn't sounded cynical or prickly. She simply sounded honest. Someone who took an honest view of themselves and of the world, as much as possible. And this honesty, over the course of breakfast, quieted Marina's earlier, tugging resentment.

They had no definite plan or schedule to follow, only a loose need to accomplish what they'd come here to do.

Did any of them ski? Holly asked. Just a couple of times in her life, Justine answered. Including the long-ago weekend with James when she was a child.

"Because we could, if we wanted," Holly continued. "It's a thing we could do. Though I haven't been skiing in years."

Marina, probably the most experienced skier in the room, imagined the three of them showing up to the nearby mountain resort, benign aliens touching down on Earth, hapless and furtive. She reminded Holly that nobody had packed the right clothes. Right, Holly acknowledged, admitting that the suggestion was something of a stalling tactic. Or not so much about stalling as setting the mood. Did the day have to be one of solemnity? It seemed that it would be, if they oriented it only around scattering the ashes.

But stalling, nonetheless. They weren't quite prepared to do what they'd come here to do. And according to Justine's phone, the weather would hold throughout the weekend. They could do it tomorrow, if they wished. They were at liberty, at their own discretion.

There'd been an old general store, Justine remembered, along the stretch of paved road. Why didn't they head out for a walk and go there, just to check it out? To see if it was even still in existence. Holly thought it was, based on what the vacation rental site had described.

Still in existence, it turned out, and open. Still that scent—of cardboard and fire and pine. If any number of other things had changed about the place, Justine couldn't tell. Three narrow aisles of choice groceries to navigate— concessions to "gourmet" tastes seemed to have been made only in relation to the chocolate and coffee selections. Justine heard the floorboards creak as Holly and Marina wandered.

Did this mark a terminal point for the three of them? Once they laid James to rest, or however you put it, would they continue to be in each other's lives? Justine wondered. With this no longer in the future, what would their communication look like? She wanted them to be in one another's lives, though she knew how these things so often went, all intentions aside.

"Can I help you find anything?" The woman who asked was probably a few years older than Holly.

"I think I'm all set," said Justine. "I just . . . I was here a long time ago."

"So was I." The woman laughed, bringing Justine's attention closer. Justine took in the flannel shirt over a turtleneck, hair cut in a short gray bob, a face of fine features, cross-hatched with fine lines like the palm of a hand. Pushed up sleeves that revealed a few silver bracelets.

"How long have you worked here?" Justine asked.

"We've owned it since the eighties, me and my partner."

She thought of asking the woman if she'd known the Kanes; it seemed within the realm of possibility, but why bring them up? Instead, she commended the woman—*that's so great*—on the longevity of the place, imagining the woman and her partner had moved here from a city in an exit-from-the-rat-race pursuit. A whole swift, potted history came to her—the woman had been a rising, power-suited executive in the financial industry, her partner a hard-charging chef—and she dismissed it as quickly.

Holly and Marina rounded the corner of the adjacent aisle, joining them, and Justine had the stray thought that Holly and the woman should know each other, by virtue of . . . what? Their age? It didn't make any sense, but still, there seemed to be something immediately linking them, at least in Justine's mind. And she realized what it was: that there existed a very subtle antagonism and wariness between the woman and

Holly, manifesting itself with no more than a slight change in the air around the four of them. And it did have something to do with age, the comparisons you instinctively draw among your cohort but don't apply to those decidedly younger or older than you. Even when the overarching mood was friendliness and good feeling, it was hard to completely avoid an element of defensiveness and territoriality. This is how you've gone about your life and that is how I've gone about mine. Did the drive toward comparison ever stop?

Sherry was the woman's name, which didn't fit with Justine's idea of her. But Sherry had introduced herself by name to Holly, as if intuiting a certain social hierarchy, chieftain to chieftain. That whatever their group was (a coven? a folk music trio on vacation?) Holly was the leader. Justine knew this to be true, despite what Holly might say or think.

It was a minor exchange with Sherry, who moved back behind the counter and quickly eased into cordiality with Holly, welcoming them to Vermont. And they, in return, complimented the entire state and Sherry's general store, and then Marina paid for the fancy chocolate bars in her hand and they headed back to the house. Uphill and down. The cold air and their panting breath. Silence and conversation.

"How old is your son, again?" Holly asked Justine. Holly walking in the middle, a younger woman to each side.

"He's three. Almost four."

"I have this client. I won't get into specifics, but he's got a newborn. He was worried, in several different directions, about becoming a father. I think they're going to be okay. But it was hard for me, having lost my sister and then losing James, to sit there and listen to him talk about this family he was creating. I thought maybe I wasn't the right therapist for him at that moment and I should recommend someone else. But now I think we were a good fit. Are a good fit. That I've been good for him and he's been good for me."

"Did you ever . . ." Justine started. She knew the sensitivity of the subject. "I don't know . . ."

"What? You can ask."

"Did you ever want to have children?"

Holly took a moment. Marina listened closely.

"I didn't *not* want them, but no. I never prioritized it in a way that might've made it happen. I never prioritized having priorities. Not in the right way."

"Prioritized having priorities," said Justine while Marina, at the same time, overlapping, asked: "There's a right way?"

"Well, that's just it. I don't know that there *is* a right way, but there's certainly that *sense* that there's a right way, and that there is a risk you take in doing it wrong."

"A risk of regret?" Justine asked.

"Regret. Or worse. Sometimes, because of what I do for work, people probably imagine I have the answers. But I don't. I just have a lot of questions. If I can ask them in a productive way, it can be useful. So, if I'd been better at priorities, who knows? I might have gotten further as a dancer, but I might never have moved back to Boston, and I wouldn't have had James in my life in the way that I did. I spent a lot of time with him when he was growing up. And then we became close again when Lila was dying."

They moved to the side of the road as a vehicle passed, then moved back and into their talk again.

"Marina took me to see the picture Alex Greenman took of you," said Justine.

"She did." Holly's way of making statements that were also questions.

Holly turned to Marina and when she turned back, Justine discerned a blush come over Holly, though it could have been the cold that colored her cheeks.

"I did," said Marina. "You know I love that picture."

"My husband loves Alex Greenman's work," said Justine. "And I was thinking I should show it to him, because I'm not actually sure he's ever seen that shot. But I keep hesitating. Like it's not for him. Like the experience of it shouldn't belong to him. And I feel strange saying that, and not wanting to share it with him, but it's true."

"You don't have to share me," said Holly, with a frosty exhalation. "I'm okay with that."

Throughout the day, they kept telling each other they should pace themselves. A square or two of the dark chocolate at a time. That's really all you need. Nobody could have said who kept going back to break off more, or when, but the bars were gone completely by the next morning and nobody voiced any grievance about not getting their fair share.

Sunday morning, early enough that the neighbors, if they were around, would still be sleeping. They might have the frozen lake all to themselves.

If not now, when? Holly thought. *How Jewish of me.*

They bundled up and pulled on their boots. Justine opened the sliding door that led onto a deck and down a slope of land to the shoreline, which could still be distinguished beneath the snow. To the left of where they stood, an ice rink had been cleared.

"Can we go out beyond it?" asked Justine. "Did he say where, exactly, we should do this?"

"No, nothing that specific," said Holly. "But let's keep moving."

None of them knew the protocol for trudging over a frozen lake, what to be aware of, to watch or listen for. What James would have known.

"There," said Holly, pointing to a sheltered area not too far from the perimeter, where the trees created a small cove and there were no houses. "That looks good to me. I'm not sure we're technically allowed to do it on the water, though I don't know if it makes a difference now that it's frozen. Figuring it all out was a lot of bureaucracy I didn't want to deal with." Justine and Marina nodded.

They walked single file: Holly, Marina, Justine. From a distance, they were a soundless, small, dark procession in a large white space. Up close, they could hear their own exhalations, see their breath circling like smoke. They walked against a wind, but it wasn't too harsh.

"Are we supposed to say something?" asked Marina, when they reached the chosen spot.

"If you want," replied Holly. "If you have something to say. But I don't think we have to."

Not one of them had something to say. Just as they hadn't had anything to say at the memorial. Perhaps speeches were not the way they conceived of their own grief and weren't consoling to them, anyway.

"We should wait for the wind to pick up again, though," said Justine, not wanting the ashes to fall unceremoniously in a sad pile, to make an ashtray of the ground.

"Good thinking," said Holly.

They stood, waiting, quiet. And when the wind returned, Holly turned her back to it, and began to shake out the urn over a patch of land between the pines, the ashes like shadow snow.

It was Lila she was thinking of. A weekend home when she lived in New York and was sleeping sometimes with Alex Greenman and was dancing professionally, and Lila was pregnant. Holly couldn't imagine being pregnant, demanding that of her own body just then. Or maybe ever. But Lila seemed at peace, content, even though there was so much to worry about. You're like the Sea of Tranquility, Holly had said to her—the moon basin they learned about as children. All lunar and tidal and powerful and feminine. Hardly, Lila had said, sitting in a chair in the small kitchen of her ground-floor apartment. They could both see that she wasn't a wreck, as Holly imagined she would be herself, in Lila's position. But then Holly also understood that she wouldn't be in Lila's position. She would have made different choices.

And then, perhaps because somber situations had long made Holly self-conscious, made her fear she couldn't be properly somber, caused her to suppress nervous laughter (she'd turned that into something of a tool in therapy, her laughter disarmed her clients), she thought of James, when Lila was dying, saying *Just compost me! Like a fucking banana peel.*

She had to stand the urn on the ground, for a moment, to wipe her wet face. She hadn't even felt it coming on. Justine's hand on her arm. Marina picking up the urn to continue until it was empty.

The trees seemed to have grown taller in the time they'd stood there. Maybe it was the change in the light, the position of the sun, the clouds, that caused Holly's shift in perspective, her sense of smallness within a vastness. Not a disorienting, depressing sensation, but rather one of being in tune with the vastness, a vital part of it. An ongoingness you might want to feel at such a moment. What James had once experienced here. And actually feeling something she thought she ought to feel made her tear up again. She missed Lila and she missed James so very much.

Marina said her name—apparently, she had said it more than once—before asking if they should go, if Holly was ready to head back. And she was, if she ever would be, so they retraced their path, now under a changing sky. They didn't talk and in the quiet Holly watched Justine and Marina trudging along in front of her, looking at them in wonder and gratitude, at how they came to be with her just then, in these winter woods.

On coming back to New York, long after dropping off Holly and soon after taking Justine home, Marina drove the rental car to Rafael's. She knew they ought to talk about James, discuss how the weekend had gone, but she wanted Rafael to intuit that if she'd wanted to talk, she could have called him on the phone, from her place. She'd driven all day, she had to work the next morning, going to her own home would have made more sense. It wasn't sense or reason she was after.

She wanted him to undress her, she wanted to tell him what to do and have him do it. She wanted sex that was like sex with James, that recalled him in some way, but also that was nothing like sex with James. James was still there in a way, and however perversely, that presence or that absence seemed necessary. She wanted sex to contain all of her contradictory impulses. Was that asking too much of sex? Of Rafael? He didn't seem to think so. She told him what she wanted, what to do, and he did it.

"What do you want?" she asked. He was inside of her now.

"This," he said.

Maybe she would get a different answer after, or in the morning, if either of them brought it up, what they wanted, how they wanted this to be. Maybe.

She stayed, they slept, and he continued sleeping as the sun came up and she left. In the stairwell, the sunlight caught her eye. Instead of descending, she took the stairs up one flight to the top, under a skylight where the winter sun came through a glass pane crisscrossed with wire. Standing in the brightness, she was instantly and seamlessly lifted from her own world and dropped into another one. It looked just like this one except the cast of light was different. As the light differs from one city to another, one coast to another. A splitting inside of her, or outside of her. In one world, in one version of her day, she continued to stand there, and time no longer adhered. In another version, she took a breath, walked down the stairs, out onto the sidewalk and into the day.

ALEX GREENMAN HAD ORGANIZED the show. The gallery had already sent out press materials. Holly would go to New York to attend the opening. She'd planned to stay with Marina this time around, or at Marina's place, since Marina would stay at Rafael's apartment, where she now spent so many of her nights. Justine had said she wouldn't miss it. Couldn't wait. Over a year had passed since they'd all seen each other, since their trip to scatter James's ashes in Vermont.

Holly had been anticipating the event, if not exactly looking forward to it. Alex, Holly thought when she first heard about the exhibition, had made his claim on James's work. He made James's work belong to him. Not literally, he hadn't purchased it, but in the way of an imprimatur, an alignment. Or an affinity. An annexation? No, not that extreme and not nearly that martial. But still. He'd taken some ownership of a vague, posthumous thing Holly hadn't even thought to possess. Because it wasn't a thing, per se, and she didn't think in terms of legacy. When Alex told her of his plans—he'd told her, he hadn't really asked, even though he was *technically* asking her, because Holly now oversaw James's estate—her first reaction wasn't *Oh how wonderful, what a great idea*. It was a sense of loss. Of discovering something had been taken from her or was in the process of being filched while she was distracted and looking the other way. Further reflection tempered this, and she knew she wouldn't have had the wherewithal or even the desire to put together anything similar. Even after all this time, or maybe because all this time had passed—the years between her and Alex, their attraction to each other over the course of those years—she understood that Alex's genuine wish to support another person (or that person's legacy) couldn't be separated from what might benefit him. What she saw as calculation for personal gain, he saw as simply being, moving around in the world. And though she admired James's work, wanted it to be seen and known, the work wasn't James. Seeing his photographs on the walls of a gallery, or even in a book, wouldn't bring him any closer to her.

Though she was eager to see Marina and Justine, even that came shaded with some unease. To see them would upset a routine she'd settled into since they'd parted ways. A routine that enabled her to live her life without always thinking that she was living the rest of her life without Lila or James. The anxiousness had to do with seeing Marina and Justine, engaging with their physical presence, whereas ("Whereas!" Eight-year-old James on a stool by a lunch counter, learning language) communication with them hadn't had that effect on her. She'd corresponded briefly with Justine around the holidays. And Marina had called, every few weeks after Vermont, and then every so often. Recently she had emailed, asking if the offer still stood, if Holly was still willing to read something she had written. Holly had said Yes! Please! Of course! Marina had yet to follow up. Holly would wait until Marina was ready, though she wished Marina wouldn't take too long. Wished she could transmit a sense of urgency to her; nothing manic or agitated, just a steady pulse: *now.* If not now, when?

The show was scheduled to open in mid-April. By the end of February, events and conferences were just beginning to be cancelled in the wave that would crest in a couple of weeks, bringing life to a halt, and a combination of stagnation and frenzy would set in as the pandemic took hold.

Nothing would be the same, you kept hearing. Everything had changed, changed utterly. And yet, had it? Holly was not at all surprised to hear that Alex was calling her from his second home up the Hudson River, having fled Manhattan immediately along with everyone else who could afford to. Of course, that's what he would have done and where he would be. Of course. The more things change . . . And he knew it, too.

He said, "Well, we're in the high-risk category, we had to get out of there." But he couldn't keep a sheepishness out of his voice. "Where are you?" he asked.

"Here, in my condo with my cat," she said. "I don't have somewhere else to go. But it's fine here. At least for now." Sarah and Everett, her solicitous young neighbors, had been checking in even before people began isolating—months ago they had invited her to dinner, she had invited them—and now they were isolating together, essentially. They formed what was being called a pod.

If Alex was going, out of habit, to invite her to shelter with them at their country house—she'd been there before one summer, sat outside with him on a deck overlooking grassy grounds, the wild, native gardens Susan tended, a pond even—he checked himself before extending the offer. Some things didn't stay the same after all.

"Good," he said. "As long as you're safe. And you're working?"

She was working still, speaking to patients on the phone or online. It was a particularly trying time for Carl, who now had very little recourse in eluding Sasquatch's footsteps; he'd been laid-off and had therefore become the primary caregiver of their active sixteen-month-old who needed near-constant attention. He called Holly on the street from his car, his one escape, while his daughter napped, and he spoke with her at least twice a week, at a reduced rate.

"Good," said Alex. Was he waiting for her to ask him if he was working or how his work was going? She assumed that photographers couldn't go out and shoot as they normally would. But did Alex really go out and shoot much anymore?

He probably had a retrospective book an art publisher was bringing out, that he had to choose images for or something, write an introduction about his past and his influences and all that. Fascinating. Any yet, and also, and still: fascinating—without sarcasm. It fascinated her. It did. His work, and what it had meant to her, and what he had meant to her, and what she had meant to him.

"Have you heard any more about the show for James?" she asked. "Are they still postponing it or totally canceling it?"

"Postponing, last I heard. Though I have no clue about timing. I'm not sure anyone really knows what's going to happen."

Holly took her phone to the couch, by the windows of her living room that looked out onto a gray and chilly afternoon in early spring.

"No," she said, settling in, her black cat in her lap. "I don't suppose anybody does."

THREE TIMES IN HIS LIFE he'd said he was happy. He must have said it, out loud, more often than that, though maybe not. In any case, there were three times he distinctly remembered. Once with Justine at a dingy bar in the East Village. Once with Holly, when his mother was in the hospital. And the third was with Marina, in a hotel room along the coast, where the sun came through blindingly white, where they kept the windows open but the linen curtains drawn during the day and moved around each other, or barely moved at all, in the half-light and the breeze from the sea.

ACKNOWLEDGMENTS

Thank you to Kate Garrick, Maryse Meijer, Kathleen Rooney, Carlene Bauer, Stephanie Feldman, Matthew Specktor, Ayşegül Savaş, Sam Lipsyte, Leigh Jurecka, Pamela Jones, Rebecca Shapiro, Emily Votruba, and Lindsay Lake. Love and gratitude to Lewis McVey and Callum McVey.

ABOUT THE AUTHOR

Deborah Shapiro is a writer in Chicago. She is the author of the novels *The Sun in Your Eyes* and *The Summer Demands*.

www.deborah-shapiro.com